The Scream of the Hawk

D1213459

ORCA BOOK PUBLISHERS

National Library of Canada Cataloguing in Publication Data

Belgue, Nancy, 1951-

Scream of the hawk / Nancy Belgue.

ISBN 1-55143-257-9

I. Title.

PS8553.E4427S37 2003   jC813'.6   C2003-910854-6

PZ7.B44Sc 2003

First published in the United States, 2003

Library of Congress Control Number: 2003107095

Summary: Lissa is unhappy with her mother's move to Ontario and now she has to look after a strange boy who keeps a hawk in a cage down by the lake.

Orca Book Publishers gratefully acknowledges the support for its publishing programs provided by the following agencies: the Government of Canada through the Book Publishing Industry Development Program (BPIDP), the Canada Council for the Arts, and the British Columbia Arts Council.

Cover design: Christine Toller
Cover illustration: eyewire.com
Printed and bound in Canada

05 04 03 • 5 4 3 2 1

IN CANADA:
Orca Book Publishers
1030 North Park Street
Victoria, BC Canada
V8T 1C6

IN THE UNITED STATES:
Orca Book Publishers
PO Box 468
Custer, WA USA
98240-0468

For my mother, Doris Hobbs McInnis,
who thought of moving as a great way to make
new friends.

Chapter One

Lissa's mom stood in the front doorway, twisting her purse in her hands. "Are you sure you don't want to come and get groceries with me?" she asked.

"No! I told you already. I'd rather stay here," Lissa said. She squinched down on the top step, picked up her mystery novel, *The Secret in the Belfry*, and flipped to page twenty-five.

"We can go for an ice cream cone."

"No thanks."

"Lissa, are you sure? We could look at bathing suits. Mrs. Maxwell from next door said you could come over and go swimming any time." From the house next door, Lissa could hear kids splashing in a swimming pool. She wished she were swimming because it was hot and sticky in Ontario, much hotter than it ever got in Victoria where ocean breezes kept the air cool all year round. Even though school started next week, it was still so hot it felt like July. Lissa missed the cool ocean breezes of the West Coast and the mountains that shimmered like meringues at the edge of the water. Southern Ontario, where she'd been living for three weeks now, was flat and hot and boring.

"It would be a great way to get to know some of the neighbors, honey," said her mom. "It's all right," Lissa said. "I'd rather stay here and read."

Her mom hesitated, then jingled her car keys. "Okay," she said. Her voice sounded sad. Lissa didn't care. She wanted her mom to feel sad. She wanted her mom to feel exactly the way she did.

"See you later then, sweetie," her mom said, stooping to give Lissa a kiss. "Maybe I'll get some ice cream and bring it home, and we can have a bowl under the tree in the back yard."

"Whatever," Lissa muttered under her breath.

She didn't even look up when her mom backed the car down the driveway.

Lissa hated her new house. She especially didn't like her next door neighbor, Carrie, or Carrie's best friend, Sophie. On the day she moved in, Carrie and Sophie had watched the movers carry Lissa's furniture up the front walk. Muggsy had bounded over to Carrie's house, sniffing happily and waving his tail.

Carrie had shrieked. "That is the ugliest dog I've ever seen," she said.

Neither girl had even said hello when Lissa had gone over to take Muggsy away. They had gone in the house and slammed the door.

There was no doubt about it. Moving was even worse than she had ever imagined it would be.

Thinking about Carrie and Sophie made Lissa miss Danielle so much she felt like there was a big fist squeezing her heart. She wondered what Danielle was doing now and fingered the silver medallion that she wore on a chain around her neck. Danielle had one just like it; they'd given them to each other on the day Lissa moved away. Lissa's medallion had the word "best" engraved on it and Danielle's had "friend." Lissa knew she was never going to have another friend that she loved as much as she loved Danielle. The thought made her scowl and squeeze her eyes together so a tear wouldn't fall on her book.

She and Danielle had been best friends since they were both six years old and in kindergarten together. Now Danielle lived in British Columbia and Lissa lived in Ontario, and Lissa just knew they were never going to see each other ever again despite all the promises her mother had made about going back to visit. Lissa's mom wasn't great at keeping promises. After all, when Lissa's parents got divorced two years ago, her mom had promised Lissa that she'd still see her dad all the time.

That hadn't turned out to be true. At first Lissa had spent every weekend with her dad. Then things changed, and she started going less and less. Lissa's mom said it was because her dad traveled a lot for business, but Lissa figured it was because her dad didn't like her as much as he did when they lived in the same house all the time.

That's what happened when parents got divorced. You lost your dad and your best friend at the same time. Now Lissa felt like she'd lost her mom too. That was because of Bill. Her mom had met Bill one evening when she was on duty in the hospital's emergency room. She had helped the doctor set Bill's broken ankle. In no time at all, Mom had told Lissa that she was getting married and since her husband-to-be had been offered a job in another city, they'd be moving. She hadn't told Lissa that the move was going to be far, far away from everything and everyone Lissa loved.

No, Mom definitely had a problem with communication.

"Hi," said a voice from the sidewalk.

Lissa squinted. She didn't want anyone to think she might be crying.

"What's the matter? Have you got something in your eye?"

"No," Lissa snapped. "Who are you?" She'd given up even trying to be nice.

"I live down the street. My name's Otis."

Otis was just a little kid, for Pete's sake. "Who'd give a kid a name like Otis?"

Lissa didn't realize she'd spoken out loud until Otis said, "My mom named me after someone called Otis Redding. He was a singer."

"How old are you?" Lissa asked. Otis didn't look very big, but he had a serious way of talking and big round glasses that made him look smart. Even on this hot day, he was wearing a cape like a miniature magician.

"I'm eight. How old are you?" Otis pushed his glasses back up his nose. They slid right back down.

"Eleven," Lissa said.

"Look what I got," said Otis. He held out his hand.

Lissa shrank back a little. Was he going to trick her with a springy, sproingy rubber snake? Or maybe even a real live bug? Lissa hated bugs, especially spiders.

"What's the matter?" asked Otis.

"Er, nothing. What've you got there, anyway?" she said. She was beginning to wish Otis would go back home.

"Take a look." Otis brought his hand closer.

It was a feather — a large tawny feather with a red tip. "Where'd you get it?" she asked.

"Come with me and I'll show you," Otis said. Lissa hesitated. Was this kid as strange as he looked?

The splashing got louder and voices carried across the warm air.

"Hey Carrie, do a handstand," someone shouted.

"I'm going to cannonball you!" yelled another. A plume of water that looked like a geyser erupted from behind the fence.

Otis looked at Lissa. Lissa looked at Otis's outstretched hand. So what if he was a weird little kid?

"Okay," she said. "Let's go."

Otis closed his fist around the feather. "Follow me," he said.

"Just exactly where do you live, anyway?" Lissa asked as she followed Otis across the street.

"I told you. There." He pointed three houses down at a big white house with a turret.

"Do you have any brothers or sisters?" Maybe there was an older kid in the family. Someone she could be friends with.

"Nope. Just me and my dad."

"Where's your mom?"

"Shhhhhhh!" Otis said. He looked up and down the street. "That's what I'm going to show you!"

This is getting weirder and weirder, thought Lissa. "Uh, maybe I should be getting back," she said, looking up at the turret and wondering if she'd been reading too many mysteries. Suddenly the big white house looked like a haunted mansion and Otis like a scary bug with big goggle eyes.

The front yard, which was tangled with weeds and overgrown bushes, seemed to go on forever. Otis tugged at her sleeve. "We have to go around to the back door," he whispered.

"Why?" Lissa asked. Her knees were beginning to feel like sponges. A fluttery feeling batted at the edges of her stomach.

"I *told* you," Otis said again. "You'll see!"

Maybe this wasn't a good idea. What did she know about this kid, after all? Maybe he had bags full of dead spiders up in that turret. Or butterflies stuck to corkboards. Or something worse. Like preserved eyeballs. He looked like the crazy scientist type with his thick glasses, his sticky-uppy black hair, his baggy shorts and the cape that practically hit his ankles.

"So, where's your dad?" Lissa asked.

"At work," Otis said. "Where else?"

Lissa sat down beside a hedge of lilac bushes. From her spot on the ground, the house looked like a gigantic castle with gingerbread trim around the roof. The curtains were drawn and a few stones were loose at the foundation. A sudden breeze turned the leaves on the lilac trees inside out. Lissa felt a drop of rain. The sounds of the kids swimming in the pool seemed a long, long way off. Otis plunked himself down beside her, his cape puddling around him.

"What's the matter?"

"It's Saturday," Lissa said. "Does your dad work on Saturdays?"

"My dad," Otis said, looking at her as if she were crazy, "works all the time."

"So, who looks after you when he's at work?"

"He does."

"Do you always talk in riddles?" Lissa asked.

"He works over there." Otis pointed to a garage with a second story. "He's a writer."

The garage was set back behind the house and surrounded by giant trees that were so thick Lissa could hardly see where Otis was pointing. It looked like a good place to hide dead bodies. In *Doves of the Dark*, one of her favorite books, the evil caretaker had buried all his victims under the stone floor of the carriage house.

"Are you coming or what?" Otis said, tugging at her arm.

"I didn't tell my mom where I was going," Lissa said. She was not setting foot in that house. Any minute bats would come flying out of the turret. Or worse, mummies would come struggling out of the storm cellar.

"Don't you like me?" Otis asked, staring at the turret.

"Of course I like you," Lissa said. "I just don't really know you." Had she heard a noise over by the back stoop?

"Well, I'm going to show you a really big secret so you can get to know me."

A cloud passed overhead. The trees rustled again and the rain pelted even harder through the leaves. A lightning bolt streaked across the sky. Seconds later a crash of thunder shook the ground. Lissa still wasn't used to the sudden way thunderstorms came up in

Ontario. Thunder and lightning hardly ever happened in Victoria. Lissa's mom had told her that the extreme heat that built up in Ontario was the reason for these storms. Lissa looked at Otis. The thunder didn't seem to bother him, but Muggsy was deathly afraid of thunder. He was a West Coast dog and didn't have much experience with big booming noises.

Muggsy was home alone, the perfect excuse, and Lissa grabbed it. "Look, I have to go," she told Otis. "My dog is likely to chew his way through the screen door when he hears this thunder. See you later!"

She sprinted across the steaming, musty smelling street, grabbed her book from the step and slammed through the screen door.

"Muggsy!" she called, heading down the hall toward the kitchen. "Where are you?"

Muggsy wasn't answering, so Lissa got down on her hands and knees and crawled around the house, looking under all the furniture. She finally discovered him hiding under the bed in Mom and Bill's room. All she could see were a pair of moist brown eyes that looked sad and terrified. Lissa crawled under the bed and put her arm around

Muggsy's neck. His hot breath dampened her cheek and his shivering body felt like the earth tremors that had shaken the ground once when she was living in Victoria. "Don't worry, Muggsy," Lissa said. "It's just a loud noise. It won't hurt you."

A boom as loud as a plane breaking the sound barrier threatened to lift the roof off the house, and Lissa grabbed Muggsy and pressed her face against his ear. A great big tear trickled down her nose and dampened Muggsy's fur.

"I don't like thunderstorms either," Lissa whispered as another tear fell. And another.

Muggsy licked her cheek in agreement. There was a damp spot under his muzzle. His panting had left a puddle of drool on the floor, but his nose was dry and hot.

"And I don't like living here," Lissa said. "And I want to go home."

Chapter Two

A car crunched the gravel in the driveway and the next minute footsteps clumped hollowly across the porch.

"Anybody home?" Bill called as the screen door slammed behind him. "Rhonda? Melissa? Muggsy?"

"In here," Lissa called back. She scurried out from under the bed. In spite of her coaxing, Muggsy wouldn't budge. She smoothed her hair and hoped her eyes wouldn't give her away.

Bill stood in the door to his room. "What're you doing in here?"

"Muggsy's under the bed."

"Uh oh." He got down on his knees and lifted the bed skirt. "Hey boy," he said in a soft, gentle voice. "I guess the thunder scared you just a little bit." Bill sat back on his haunches and looked carefully at Lissa. "Where's your mom?"

"She went for groceries."

"Thunderstorms can be real scary," he said. "I used to hate them when I was your age. My brother and I thought it sounded like a hundred planes were breaking the sound barrier all at once. We even used to wear ear-muffs. In July!"

The rain had slowed to a gentle patter and the air coming in through the open window felt ten degrees cooler.

"The heat's finally broken," Bill said. "Come on," he held out his hand to Lissa, but let it fall when she didn't take it. "Let's make some tea."

Something cold and wet touched Lissa's ankle. She looked down. The tip of Muggsy's nose was poking out from under the bed.

"Even Muggsy's recovering," Bill said, laughing. "Now, how about that tea?"

Lissa nodded. "Come on, Muggsy."

"What did you do today?" Bill asked as he put the kettle on to boil. "Once the storm hit, the golfing was a wash-out."

"Nothing." Lissa didn't think going to Otis's house really counted. After all, she'd come home before she'd set foot inside the door.

Bill rattled around getting out milk and sugar. He set some mugs on the table. "I'd be happy to sign you up for some golf lessons."

Lissa shook her head. She didn't want to play golf.

Her mom's car pulled into the driveway. Lissa went to the window and watched her mom sprint across the wet grass. Behind her Bill put out another mug.

"Hi, you guys," Mom said, coming in the back door. "Boy, did that storm come up quickly. A tree was hit by lightning up on Main Street and a huge branch fell into the drugstore window. Traffic was completely blocked. Sorry I couldn't get home sooner. Are you okay?" She hugged her daughter.

Bill gave Mom a squeeze. Lissa reached down and scratched Muggsy's ears so she wouldn't have to see the way Mom always lit up like a birthday cake whenever Bill was around. She didn't remember her mom ever looking that way at her dad.

"Muggsy was scared."

"Poor old Muggsy," said Mom.

Muggsy wagged his shaggy white tail. It must be great to be a dog, thought Lissa.

They sipped in silence while the rain fell gently on the window. When it let up, Bill went out to bring the groceries in from the car and Mom reached over and gave Lissa's hand a pat.

"I moved a lot when I was growing up. I know you miss everyone in Victoria, but you'll make new friends here. You'll see. It just takes time."

"Everyone here is mean."

"There are nice people everywhere, hon."

"They make fun of me."

"Ignore those kids. Find the ones that you like."

"There aren't any."

Her mom was about to say something more when Bill shouldered through the door, five plastic grocery bags hanging from each hand.

"Whew! Just in time. Looks like another storm cloud's moving in."

The wind sent a beach ball careening across the yard.

Lissa put her mug in the sink and escaped to her room She hated it when Mom tried to tell her how she'd make friends and how she'd moved all the time growing up. Mom was pretty. She had long brown hair and blue eyes. Bill looked at her with a soft goofy expression on his face. Lissa's hair was red and curly, and as if that wasn't bad enough, she was getting pimples and had to wear big baggy sweaters so no one would see how much weight she'd gained.

Besides, Mom had Bill, and Lissa didn't have anybody.

Mom had followed her to her room. She came in and sat on the bed. Lissa wanted to holler at her mother to go away, but the look on her mom's face stopped her. She looked worried and a little older. Tiny lines in the corners of her eyes didn't go away when she stopped smiling. Her blue eyes were grayer than usual.

She put out her hand and smoothed Lissa's red curls. Lissa liked it when Mom stroked her hair. She heaved a deep sigh and closed her eyes. If she tried hard enough she could almost believe she was still in her room in Victoria and Danielle was going to be coming over soon for a sleepover and everything was just as it had always been.

"Bill and I thought we'd all go to the Harrow Fall Fair tomorrow," said Mom, breaking into Lissa's daydream. "Why don't you invite Carrie Maxwell from next door to come with us?"

"Mo-o-o-om," said Lissa. "I don't want to invite her."

Soon after she'd moved in, Lissa had tried to make friends. Even though she'd heard Carrie and Sophie's mean remarks about Muggsy, she'd knocked on Carrie's door just as her mother had suggested, but Carrie had gone to sleep over at Sophie's house. The next morning, Lissa saw her standing on the corner talking to Sophie and two boys from the house around the corner. They ran off when they saw her coming, Lissa was sure of it. Carrie and Sophie were always talking and laughing. They sat next to each other at the beach and ate lunch together and never even looked her way.

"Perhaps if I talked to Mrs. Maxwell, she . . ."

"*No!*" Lissa shrieked. The thought made

her bury her head under the pillows. She didn't care if her mother looked tired and worried. She was never, never, *never*, going to be friends with Carrie Maxwell and that was that!

Lissa stayed in her room and read until Mom called her for supper. After supper, she went back to her room and read until she fell asleep with the lights on.

The next morning after breakfast Bill, Mom and Lissa set out for the fair. Lissa moped around the fairgrounds, watching all the kids with big families: aunts, uncles, brothers and sisters. A boy and girl poked at each other until their father came over, took the boy by the hand and picked up the little girl. Lissa thought of her dad three thousand miles away in Victoria.

In the animal exhibition building, Lissa looked at the cows with their big brown eyes and at the tiny sheep that were curled up beside their mother. Even the animals had real families! Bill and Mom trailed behind. At the pie tent, Mom pointed out the prize-winning elderberry pie. Lissa wrinkled her nose. Elderberry pie. What were elderberries, anyway?

"You look like you need convincing. Would you like to try some?" asked a lady sitting behind the table.

"Go on, Lissa. Try it," said Mom.

Lissa shook her head. "No thanks."

"Rhonda, Lissa," Bill called. "Come and see this giant pumpkin. It says here it weighs 639 pounds!"

"Coming!" Mom said. "Come on, Lissa."

"In a minute," Lissa said.

"I'll try some," said a familiar voice.

Lissa turned around. There stood Otis, his big googly glasses balanced on the tip of his nose, his crazy magician's cape dragging on the ground behind him. "Hi Lissa," he said as he dropped some money onto the table. "Want a bite?" He held out a forkful of pie. "It's kind of like blueberry."

A long-legged man wearing thick glasses came up behind Otis. He reminded Lissa of the giant blue herons she had seen picking their way along the shores of the marsh and the lake.

"Otis," said the man, "who is your friend?"

"This is Lissa. She lives in the big brick house across the street."

"Hi, Lissa," said the man. "You must have moved into the Nixon place."

"I guess so," Lissa said. She hadn't heard the house called that before.

"I'm Otis's dad," continued the man.

Lissa nodded.

"How are you liking Harmony Beach?"

"It's okay . . ."

"I'm Rhonda Connors," said Lissa's mom, coming over from the pumpkin display and sticking out her hand. "I didn't know Lissa and Otis were friends."

"Mo-o-o-om," Lissa said. "Otis and I just met yesterday."

"I'm Otis's father, John Striker."

"John Striker, the writer?"

"That's me."

"Bill, come here," Mom called, waving at Bill to come and join them. "I just love all your books," she said. "I've read every one."

Otis's dad looked pleased.

"Hi," Bill said. "I'm Bill Connors."

Otis poked Lissa in the ribs. "Don't worry," he said. "This happens all the time. My dad's sort of famous."

"What kind of books does he write?"

"Scary books."

Lissa looked at Otis's dad. He didn't look scary. In fact, he looked like a teacher. Of mathematics.

"Really?"

"Yeah, about ghosts and stuff like that."

"Do you ever read them?"

"Sometimes. But I like science fiction better."

"I like mysteries."

"Well, if you like mysteries, you're really going to like the secret I was going to show you yesterday."

Otis grabbed Lissa's hand. "Let's go look at the rides," he said, turning to his dad. "Can Lissa and I go to the midway?"

Lissa's mom and Bill glanced at each other.

Maybe I don't want to go, Lissa thought. Not with Willie Wonka here.

"Come on, Lissa," said Otis. "Let's ride the double Ferris wheel."

Bill and Mom and Otis's dad were already deep in conversation. Lissa folded her arms across her chest and followed Otis towards the midway, scuffing her shoes in the dirt as she went.

"We'll meet you at the grandstand in half

an hour," shouted Mr. Striker after them.

Otis chattered noisily all the way to the rides. The air smelled like fried onions, straw and cotton candy. People shrieked and laughed as the rides shot up and down, dipped and swung, twisted and twirled. In spite of herself, excitement percolated in her stomach.

"Was your dog okay?" asked Otis as they joined the line, crunching on candy apples.

"Huh?"

"Yesterday, during the storm. Remember?"

"Oh, right! Yeah, he was hiding under the bed, but he was okay."

"So, where'd you move from, anyway?"

"British Columbia."

"Wow! Part of my mom's family was from B.C. What's it like there?"

Lissa didn't want to think about her home province right now. She took a bite of her candy apple. "It's all right," she said.

Otis's eyes sparkled behind his big glasses. "We're next!" he said.

The sounds of the midway grew farther and farther away as the big wheel rotated higher and higher into the sky.

Otis rocked the seat back and forth.

"Look at the grandstand," he said. "It's the size of a Lego house."

Lissa could just make out the bright pink shirt her mom was wearing. She tried to wave, but the seat swayed and she clutched the bar in front of them.

"See how the fields look like square patches?" said Otis. "My dad says it's so flat here that you can stand in your window and watch your dog run away for two days."

Lissa smiled weakly. "Why do you always wear that cape?" she asked.

"Cause I'm a shaman."

Lissa was about to ask Otis what he meant when, with a slight jerk and a rush of carnival music, the Ferris wheel started to turn. Up, up, up went the wheel in which Lissa and Otis were sitting while at the same time their seat started to go around. It was dizzying and scary.

Kids shrieked, and Lissa closed her eyes and held on tight.

Finally the fast spinning sensation slowed down and little by little the big wheel came to a stop. Lissa and Otis were at the very top and had to wait while each seat was unloaded. Lissa sat silently, clutching the bar while Otis chattered endlessly.

"Do you want to go again? Maybe we should try the roller coaster, or look! There's a Loop the Loop. Come on, Lissa, let's ask if we can ride some more."

The adults were waiting at the exit. "Did you kids have fun?" Bill asked.

"Did we!"

Lissa managed to nod.

"We want to go on the roller coaster," Otis said.

Lissa's mom took a good long look at Lissa's face. "Sorry Otis, but we have to get going now."

"Ugh!" said Otis as if he hadn't heard. "There's Carrie Maxwell and Sophie."

Lissa looked where Otis was pointing. Carrie and Sophie were with Sophie's big brother Alex and they were coming towards them.

Lissa turned her back and hunched her shoulders, praying that her mother wouldn't say anything.

"Hi girls," said Lissa's mom.

Mo-o-o-om, Lissa thought, don't do this to me.

"Have you met Lissa?" Mom continued.

"Yeah. Hi, Lissa," said Carrie. Carrie

had blond hair and blue eyes. She looked like a Barbie doll.

Lissa wondered who was going to speak next.

"Hi, remember me?" It was Otis.

Don't let him say we just rode the Ferris wheel together, prayed Lissa.

"Lissa sure was scared up there on the Ferris wheel," Otis said. "But it was fun, right Lissa? And now we're going to ride the roller coaster."

Sophie and Carrie giggled and Alex nudged them. "Well, have fun," he said.

The three walked away, their arms linked, Sophie glancing back over her shoulder as she whispered in Carrie's ear.

Lissa's face burned. Otis didn't seem to notice anything.

What a dumb kid!

Mr. Striker came back from the food area, carrying five drinks and five boxes of French fries. "These are the best fries in the county," he said, handing a box to each person. "They make them from their home-grown potatoes and drench them in malt vinegar. There's nothing like them!"

Lissa's fries stuck in her throat. She

might as well have been eating twigs. Not only was she doomed to be the geekiest kid in town, she was obviously doomed to have the second geekiest kid as her only friend.

Chapter Three

"Did you know your friend Otis's dad was a famous writer?" asked Bill as he maneuvered *move the car* the car out of the crowded parking lot.

"Otis is *not* my friend. I just met him."

"You know what Bill means, honey," said Mom, looking at Lissa over her shoulder.

"No, I *don't* know. And I don't know anything about Otis because I just met him yesterday," Lissa snapped. Why was everyone trying to make such a big deal out of Otis anyway?

Bill and Mom exchanged another glance.

"Well, Otis seems like a really nice little guy," Bill said.

"I think he's weird," Lissa said.

"What do you mean — weird?" Mom asked.

"He keeps talking about a secret he wants to tell me. And I think that house he lives in is spooky."

Mom laughed. "He's probably got a good imagination like his father."

"That reminds me," said Bill. "Mr. Striker has a proposition for you."

Lissa watched the flat fields, dotted with orange pumpkins, slip by the window. Every mile or so a farmer had set up a stand selling vegetables and fruit. In Victoria, she and Danielle had gone to the pumpkin patch every year and bought pumpkins that they carved into scary faces.

"Aren't you curious?" asked Mom.

Sometimes they got Danielle's dad to judge the pumpkin carvings and last year he'd judged Lissa's to be the scariest. He'd taken Lissa and Danielle out for pizza afterwards. Lissa's dad had come with them. It had been one of the best nights of the whole year.

"Earth to Lissa," said Mom.

"Huh? What?"

"You sure were far away," said Mom.

Yeah, about three thousand miles, thought Lissa.

"Aren't you curious about Mr. Striker's proposition?"

Proposition, what proposition?

Bill laughed. "I think you'd better start again, Rhonda. Give Lissa a minute to catch up."

"Mr. Striker is going to be very busy for the next month or so. He's doing some research for his new book and he thought that since you and Otis hit it off so well, maybe you could watch him after school and on weekends."

"You want me to look after Otis?" asked Lissa. She was listening now, but she couldn't believe what she was hearing.

"Well, yes. I thought it would be a good way for you to earn some extra money."

"Otis is a nut case. I don't want to spend every weekend with him for a whole month!"

"That's up to you, Lissa. But I thought you might want to start a savings account."

Lissa thought about that for a minute. "How much do you think I could earn?"

"Mr. Striker said he would pay you seventy-five dollars a week. In one month you could have three hundred dollars."

Three hundred dollars was a lot of money, but Lissa couldn't see how that was going to help her make friends. Otis was the one kid nobody liked. She shook her head.

"I don't need money that badly."

"You might feel differently when you want to get some new clothes for your trip to B.C."

"What trip to B.C?"

Mom and Bill looked at each other.

"What?" asked Lissa.

"We were going to tell you tonight, but since the subject has come up . . ."

"*What?*" Lissa sat up in her seat and leaned forward.

"I talked to your dad last night, and we thought you might like to go out to visit him at Thanksgiving."

"Do you really mean it?" Lissa asked.

"Yes," said Mom with a smile. "I've already called about the cost of airfare."

Thanksgiving! Why that was only a month away.

"And if you earn one hundred dollars toward the ticket, your dad and I will pay the rest."

Lissa thought about it. One hundred for the ticket left two hundred dollars to spend on clothes. But what was she going to do every day with Otis? Would she have to hang out in his spooky house?

"You think it over, hon," her mom said. "I told Mr. Striker we'd let him know tonight. If you can't do it, he's going to have to make other arrangements. He's starting his research next week."

"Okay, I'll do it." It might not be her idea of fun, but just think! B.C.! Victoria! Fresh, salty air! The ocean! Danielle! And, best of all, Dad! Maybe she could keep the Otis part a secret from the other kids.

"You can call Mr. Striker when we get home and tell him your decision," said Mom. "He'll probably want you to come over tonight so he can show you around."

A flicker of cold ran up Lissa's spine.

She was going to have to spend a lot of time in Otis's big, spooky house.

With the weird feeling that he had pickled eyeballs stored in his attic.

And the weird way his eyes googled at her from behind his thick lenses.

And what was the secret he kept talking about?

She stared out the window and tried to convince herself that it would be worth it.

She imagined eagles soaring through the sky at Willows Beach in Victoria and thought of riding her bike along the boardwalk and picking blackberries in Uplands Park. Besides, she really didn't *know* that there were pickled eyeballs in Otis's attic. It was just a spooky feeling that wouldn't go away.

The car pulled up in front of their house. She headed for the back door without waiting for Mom or Bill.

Muggsy followed her to her room and jumped up on her bed. Lissa picked up her book and flopped down beside him. She only had two more chapters to go before it ended. Lissa always hated it when a book came to an end.

She could hear Mom and Bill rummaging around in the kitchen as they fixed dinner. Their voices carried into her room.

"So sad about that little fellow," said Mom.

Lissa's ears perked up.

"Yeah," said Bill. "That's one reason John was so anxious to hire Lissa. Otis doesn't get along that well with people. Today was the liveliest he's seen him since the accident."

"It'll be good for her too. She's been

miserable since leaving Victoria."

Lissa crept to the door where she could hear better.

"It takes time to adjust to a new place," said Bill.

"I know," said Mom. "But some people don't adapt as easily as others. I was much more outgoing than Lissa. Moving was an adventure to me."

"Lissa's adventures are in books," said Bill, laughing.

"That's exactly what I mean," said Mom. "She spends all her time reading. She's never going to make friends if she doesn't leave her room."

"Well, maybe that's why this job is such a good idea. Not only will she be out of her room, she'll be working for a writer."

The screen door slammed and Mom's and Bill's voices faded. Lissa peeked out her window. Mom and Bill were sitting under the big black walnut tree, sipping glasses of wine. Lissa sank back on her bed.

What accident?

They had fresh corn on the cob and blueberries for dinner. "That's just about the end of the season for corn," said Mom. "Weather report says there's a cold front coming down from Upper Michigan. Temperatures might be close to freezing by Wednesday."

Lissa stared out the window. It was getting dark earlier and earlier. The unseasonably hot summer weather was fading away. Winter would come soon. Her first winter in Ontario. Her first winter with snow that stayed on the ground. Her first winter away from Dad and Danielle.

Then she remembered. It was only a month until Thanksgiving.

Later, when Lissa was helping Mom with the supper dishes, she asked, "Where's Otis's mom?"

Her mother looked up from rinsing her plate. "I thought you knew," she said. "Didn't Otis tell you?"

Lissa shook her head.

"His mom was killed six months ago in an avalanche . . . "

The accident! Lissa stared at her mother.

"She was a biologist and was on an expedition in B.C. when an avalanche swept her into a lake. Neither she nor her colleagues have ever been found."

"Wow!" Lissa said. Maybe that was why

Otis walked around in a cape talking about secrets.

"His father has done everything he can to find her. He and several friends spent a whole week combing the mountain where the accident took place, but, apart from a canoe, nothing was found."

"Poor Otis!"

"That's why his dad is so pleased that Otis has you for a friend, Lissa. He's been acting strangely since the accident. He hasn't wanted to go out much. He spends a lot of time up in the turret."

Lissa rinsed a cup under hot running water. From the kitchen window, she could just make out the round white roof of the turret. A tree grew on the wide front lawn of Otis's house, a huge tree whose branches seemed to spread forever, covering the street, blocking the moon and creating gray spiky shadows on the windows.

Lissa shivered. She felt bad for Otis, but the thought of spending every afternoon and weekend in Otis's house seemed even less appealing now.

They both jumped when the phone rang.

"Lissa, it's for you," Bill called in from the living room. "It's Mr. Striker."

Lissa's heart hit her toes.

"I told him you said you'd be happy to help out," Bill continued.

Lissa picked up the phone. Behind her, her mom put dishes in the dishwasher; the friendly clatter of home made her feel better.

"Hi, Mr. Striker," Lissa said. She sipped a mouthful of tea to soothe her dry throat.

When she hung up Mom looked up expectantly.

"He wants me to come over in fifteen minutes," Lissa said.

"Well, don't be too long," Mom said with a smile. "School tomorrow."

Lissa groaned. In all the excitement, she'd almost forgotten. Tomorrow was the first day of school. More torture.

But first, she had her meeting with Mr. Striker.

"Victoria, Victoria, Victoria," she chanted under her breath as she put on her jacket.

"Bye, Mom," she hollered as she closed the screen door behind her.

Muggsy whined as if warning her not to go.

"Victoria, mountains, ocean, *Dad*," Lissa said as she took a deep breath and started down the street.

The trees rustled in the dark and, behind her, Mom shut the wooden door with a bang, blocking off the light from the kitchen.

Some of the windows in the houses farther along the block were lit with a warm yellow glow. Lissa imagined the families inside. Parents would be laughing, and kids would be getting ready for the first day of school, laying out their new clothes, washing their hair and talking on the phone to their friends. Carrie was probably making plans to meet Sophie for lunch while Lissa had to go talk to a sad kid in a haunted house.

A noise behind her made goose flesh prickle her skin. The dark, windy street was alive with shadows. As she ran up Otis's front steps, she looked back and caught a glimpse of a large, silent bird swooping low to the ground.

But there was no one else behind her; no one lurking on the dark, rustling sidewalk. There might have been no one outside in the entire town.

No one but her.

Chapter Four

"Welcome to the house of Striker," said Otis's dad as he opened the front door.

Lissa had almost turned back three times on her way over. Once when her mom had accidentally plunged her into darkness, once when a giant owl had swooped across the street and once when the doorbell clanged like a hundred church bells gone berserk.

"I must be crazy," Lissa muttered under her breath.

Mr. Striker turned from the closet where he was hanging up her coat. "Sorry, Lissa. Did you say something?"

Lissa shook her head. "Otis," yelled Mr. Striker, "Lissa's here."

Something clattered above her head, as if someone were playing marbles in the up-stairs hallway.

"That must be Otis putting away his marbles," said Mr. Striker.

Lissa blinked. Had he read her mind?

"Come on in here," he opened a many-paned glass door that led into a room lit only by a fire. "We've got the first fire of the season burning tonight," he said, switching on a table lamp. A dull yellow pool of light illuminated one corner of the room. "I was just about to start on some reading," Mr. Striker added, pointing to a pile of books beside a wing chair.

Lissa glanced furtively around the room. In the dim light, she could make out stuffed animals and birds on the mantle and mounted on the walls. She shuddered under the beady stare of a hawk that stood on top of a tall bookshelf.

Mr. Striker followed her gaze. "Don't be upset by those old relics, Lissa," he said. "Otis's grandfather was a taxidermist. These few moth-eaten treasures were all he left us in his will."

Lissa gulped. No wonder Otis was weird, living in a house like this!

"Have a seat, Lissa," said Mr. Striker, indicating a footstool in front of the fireplace.

Lissa sat down gingerly.

"I'm really pleased you could help Otis and me out," he said smiling. His beaky nose and long legs made him seem like one of the strange animals that lined the bookshelves.

Lissa managed to nod.

"All you need to do is keep Otis company while I'm working. I work in an office over the garage," he continued, "so I'm never far away, but I need extra peace and quiet for the next month while I get this book started."

Lissa nodded again.

"I've got a lot of research to do, so I may have to travel into Windsor a few times which means you and Otis would be here alone. Do you feel comfortable with that?"

"I guess so." Danielle, pumpkin carving, visiting the seals, *home*, Lissa reminded herself.

Otis arrived in the doorway. He was wearing his cape and was carrying a square black case. He looked like a traveling sorcerer.

"I've been practicing my magic tricks,"

he said, pulling a white scarf out of his sleeve. "Want to see?"

"Just a minute, Otis," Mr. Striker said. "First let's give Lissa the run down."

He stood up. "Come on Lissa, we'll show you around."

Lissa followed Mr. Striker back into the hallway, Otis bringing up the rear. The strange procession turned right and marched toward the kitchen.

"I thought I'd better show you where the food is," joked Mr. Striker. "That's the most important thing after all."

The kitchen was big and old. In the center was a wooden table scarred with deep cuts, and underneath an ancient looking dog looked up from under his shaggy eyebrows. He was huge! "That's Baskerville," said Otis. "He's ten years old."

"Baskerville is an Irish Wolfhound," said Mr. Striker. At the sound of his master's voice, Baskerville unfolded himself and stood up. His was as big as Otis!

"I used to ride on his back when I was little," said Otis.

Lissa tried to think of something to say, but her voice seemed to have lost its power.

She was afraid all she would do was squeak.

Otis was suffering Baskerville's attentions in silence. The giant dog had an equally giant tongue and he was licking Otis's face with one leisurely slurp after another.

He didn't look very scary when he did that. Otis was chuckling and Mr. Striker smiled fondly at the sight.

Lissa started to relax. Maybe this wasn't going to be as bad as she had thought. As long as Carrie and Sophie and Alex didn't find out.

"Out here is the back yard," Mr. Striker said, opening the back door. "Otis has a tree fort in the black walnut tree, but don't go up there because it's getting pretty rickety. I think we'll have to pull it down soon."

He crossed to a bulletin board beside the phone. "Here are all the important numbers, including my cell phone. If I'm not here and you need to get in touch with me, you can just call me at this number at any time. But Otis knows all this. It's not like you have to baby-sit him, really."

Lissa glanced over at Otis. He was still sitting on the floor beside Baskerville who had stopped licking and started panting. Otis grinned at her and snapped his fingers. A ping pong ball appeared from nowhere. Lissa blinked.

"Otis, save your tricks for later," said Mr. Striker. "Now, let's go upstairs." He led the way to a staircase hidden behind a wall. He stopped when he saw the look on Lissa's face. "When these old houses were built, there were always two staircases. One for the servants and one for the family. It's kind of fun, isn't it?"

Lissa looked up into the dark where the staircase curved away into the second floor. She didn't know if she'd call it fun, but it was kind of intriguing.

"And here's the playroom." Mr. Striker opened a door that led into a giant room, filled top to bottom with toys. "Otis spends a lot of time in here."

"Come on, Lissa," said Otis. "I want to show you my spider collection."

Just as she had feared! A spider collection! Any second he was going to show her his pickled eyeballs and expect her to touch one.

Mr. Striker must have seen the look on her face. "Don't worry, Lissa," he said. " It's not as bad as it seems. Otis's mother had an interest in spiders. This is a specimen collection that she had put together for the local museum of natural history. The spiders aren't alive."

Otis pulled Lissa over to a giant cabinet where an entire shelf was devoted to small terrariums containing spiders of different varieties.

"This one's a black widow," said Otis. "It was found right here in this house!"

Lissa shuddered. Otis didn't seem to notice. "My mom was interested in lots of different things," he said with a mysterious tone in his voice. "She told me that spiders are the best kind of pesticide. Someone in England figured out that every year the total weight of the insects eaten by spiders is greater than the total weight of all the people that live there! So if you don't want to be up to your eyeballs in insects, you should never kill a spider. Besides, it's bad luck."

In spite of herself, Lissa was curious. She didn't know spiders were that interesting.

"Well, that's about all you need to know, Lissa," said Mr. Striker. "Do you have any questions?"

"Does Otis have any other bug collections?" she blurted out.

Mr. Striker laughed. "No, just a few dead spiders."

That's a lot of bad luck, thought Lissa.

"I have a marble collection, though," said Otis.

"I'm going to get back to my reading," said Mr. Striker.

"Can Lissa stay for a while?" Otis was opening his magic kit. "I have a few more tricks I want to show her."

"Up to you, Lissa," said Mr. Striker. "Can you stay?"

Lissa snuck a look at the spiders in the cabinet. Maybe things wouldn't seem quite so eerie in the daylight. "I can't tonight," she said. "I have some reading to do too." That was true enough, she thought. She was on the last chapter of her current mystery and was dying to see how it finished.

"Just for a few minutes?" Otis begged.

"You heard Lissa. Not tonight, Merlin," said his dad.

Lissa felt guilty but not guilty enough to change her mind. Besides, there'd be lots of time tomorrow to see Otis's magic tricks. Tomorrow, and the day after and the day after that. She gulped.

Otis followed her downstairs. Mr. Striker

went into the library and settled himself in a chair. Lissa could see his long gangly legs sprawled out before him as he picked up a book and turned the page. He had already forgotten she was there.

Otis opened the closet door and handed Lissa her coat.

"I guess I'll see you tomorrow right after school," he said.

"Sure," said Lissa.

"And we can go down to the lake."

"The lake? Why the lake?"

"Because I have something really, really, really important to tell you."

Lissa looked at Otis. His eyes seemed huge behind his glasses. He reached over and up and said, "Presto."

Like magic, a feather appeared from behind her ear. It was the same feather he'd had in his palm two days ago.

"How did you do that?" Lissa asked, amazed. "You're really good for a little kid."

"Thanks," said Otis. "Remember what I said the other day?"

Lissa nodded. He sure was weird. She was right about that! "You mean about your secret?"

Otis nodded. "It's a really big secret."

"Does your dad know?"

Otis shook his head. "Nope. You'll be the only one."

Lissa edged toward the door.

"What kind of secret?" Lissa wasn't sure she wanted in on this secret. In her experience secrets were not always the best things. Once Danielle had told Lissa that her brother had taken twenty dollars from her mom's wallet. Danielle had made Lissa promise not to tell anyone about it because she'd been afraid her brother would tell that Danielle broke a stained glass window while playing baseball in the church parking lot. Lissa had promised. She hadn't told anyone the truth, even when Susie, Danielle's cousin, was accused of taking the money.

No, secrets could be serious business.

"Don't forget," Otis hissed as she went down the steps. "Tomorrow." And he waggled the feather and closed the door.

"What's the inside of the house like?" asked Lissa's mom when Lissa came in. "It looks huge."

"It *is* huge," Lissa said. "And it has two staircases. Mr. Striker says that one was for servants. The house was built in 1890."

"Wow," said Mom. "If walls could talk, I bet we could get a few great stories out of that place."

And how, thought Lissa.

Mom looked all excited. "Danielle's mom phoned while you were out. They are making all kinds of plans for when you come to visit. Danielle wants you to phone her so you can talk about it."

"Okay," Lissa said, thinking about the dark house and the beady-eyed stuffed animals and about Otis and his eager, unblinking eyes and the spider collection and . . .

"You don't seem very happy, hon."

"Sorry, Mom. I am. I guess I'm just tired."

"Well, go phone Danielle and get right to bed. School tomorrow, remember."

Lissa nodded. As she dialed Danielle's number she couldn't help but think about the feather.

What part did that feather play in Otis's secret?

Well, she would know soon enough.

"Hello?" said Danielle's voice on the other end of the line.

And the feather and Otis and the scary house across the street were forgotten.

Chapter Five

It was drizzling in the morning, and as Lissa packed her lunch she saw Sophie run up Carrie's front porch and knock on her door. In another minute the two girls ran down the walk under a big blue-and white-striped umbrella.

Tears stung Lissa's eyes as she remembered her talk with Danielle. At first, Danielle had told her that she and Megan had taken a picnic down to Willows Beach and gone sailing with Megan's big brother. Instead of feeling happy, Lissa had felt a whisper of jealousy. Danielle's life was going on as if Lissa had never been part of it. She was having fun with her new friend, doing all their special stuff like taking picnics to the beach, climbing the rocks and feeding the seals. It didn't sound like she missed Lissa one bit.

Then, Danielle had said, "It's not as much fun as it was when you were here, Liss," and everything had been all right.

They had talked for twenty minutes, planning all the things they would do during Lissa's visit.

Finally Lissa's mom had said, "Lissa! Time to hang up! It's ten thirty."

Lissa had found it hard to fall asleep; she had so many things to think about. They were going to take the ferry to Vancouver and see the aquarium. Danielle's mom was going to take them for tea at the Empress Hotel! Dad was going to meet her at the airport and take her out for dinner and he even promised to take them to the farmer's market on Salt Spring Island on Saturday morning. Lissa could hardly wait.

Mom looked up from her coffee. "Want a ride this morning, hon? It's lousy weather."

"Why, there's Otis," she said as she rinsed out her coffee cup. "Let's give him a lift too." Before Lissa could stop her, Mom had opened the back door and called him.

"Otis! I'm just about to drive Lissa to school. Come on in and you can come with us."

"Mo-o-o-om!" said Lissa. This was her worst nightmare. Her mom was going to drive right up to the front door of the school and drop him off.

"Yes," said Mom, turning to give Lissa a puzzled look.

"Oh, nothing." Her mother wouldn't understand. She would tell Lissa not to be unkind.

Otis appeared, dripping like a rainspout, in the back doorway. He was wearing a giant yellow slicker and a rain hat like the ones fishermen wear. Where did he find these getups? He always looked like he was dressed for Halloween.

On the way to school they passed Carrie and Sophie. Lissa's mom slowed the car. For an awful moment, Lissa thought she was going to ask them if they wanted a ride, but before she could get the window open, the girls turned up a driveway.

"Oh, look," said Mom. "I guess they're going to call on someone."

"That's Mark's house," said Otis. "Carrie has a crush on him. She thinks he's hot just because he likes skateboarding and rides a BMX."

Actually, Lissa had seen Mark biking in front of Carrie's house and thought he was hot too. But she wasn't going to let Otis or her mom know that. The car sailed by the driveway.

As they pulled up in front of the school Lissa looked around nervously. No one her age was anywhere in sight. She breathed a sigh of relief. Other cars were pulling up, and kids were jumping out and running into the school. Lissa crossed her fingers.

"Okay, let's go," she said, jumping out and slamming the door. Behind her, she could hear Otis taking his time, gathering his books and thanking her mom. Lissa was already in the school and down the hall before Otis had even shut the car door.

Carrie, Sophie and Mark came in the back entrance, dripping and laughing and talking happily. Lissa opened her locker and hung up her coat. She was getting out her books when Carrie brushed by, her long hair tumbling out of her rain hat, her backpack slung carelessly over one shoulder.

"Hi, Lissa," she said. "Do you want to walk home with Sophie and me after school?"

Lissa just about slammed her locker on her finger.

Carrie Maxwell had actually said hi to her, Lissa Reynolds. What's more, she'd invited her to . . .

"Lissa," said a voice. Lissa froze. This couldn't be happening. Slowly she looked around. There was Otis, like a wet, yellow banana, holding out a soggy paper lunch bag.

"You forgot your lunch. Your mom asked me to give it to you."

"Uh, thanks," said Lissa, taking the fraying bag from Otis's grubby fingers.

"Don't forget," he said, looking meaningfully at Carrie. "After school. Our *secret*."

He looked so eager Lissa didn't have the heart to pretend she didn't know what he was talking about.

Carrie was watching, curiosity and contempt written all over her face. The bell rang and Otis ambled away, leaving a trail of water behind him.

"You and Otis Striker have a secret?" Carrie asked, raising her eyebrows.

"It's nothing," Lissa said. She didn't even

know what the secret was!

"Well, I guess you won't be walking home with us, then. Bye, Lissa."

Carrie's blond hair swung prettily across her back as she hurried down the hall toward her classroom.

Just my luck, Lissa thought. She finally acts like I'm alive and Otis shows up babbling about his dumb secret.

"Hi, Lissa," said Alex as she sat down in her new classroom.

What was up? she wondered. Alex had never spoken to her before either.

Maybe Harmony Beach wasn't going to be such a bad place to live after all.

Alex leaned forward and tossed something across the aisle. A black furry creature landed on her science notebook. "Otis, the human insect, asked me to give you this."

Lissa screeched.

"It's a spider that fell out of your lunch bag."

Lissa's eyes filled with tears. They were teasing her.

And it was Otis's fault.

Lissa looked at the spider on her desk. It was just a fake one, made of plastic.

Alex and the others were laughing. "Otis is always talking about bugs," said Alex. "Have you checked your lunch bag? There's probably one in there for real!"

"What's going on, Alex?" said Ms. Johnson.

"Nothing."

"Lissa?" she said after checking her name on the attendance sheet.

Lissa jumped and covered the spider with her textbook. "Er, Nothing." She wasn't going to let Alex know just how miserable she felt. And she didn't want to make a bad impression on her new teacher on the first day of school.

"Well, then, class, let's pay attention."

Ms. Johnson gave Alex and Lissa a stern look then turned to the chalkboard. "To start the year off right, the class is going on a field trip to Point Pelee on Friday. We'll be leaving right after attendance is taken and will be gone all day. So it's very important that you all get these permission slips signed and returned by tomorrow. And, be sure to wear proper clothes as we'll be hiking through the woods and doing a beach clean up." Ms. Johnson's voice droned on and on . . .

Lissa's attention wandered. She felt like

a prisoner marking the days in her cell. She glanced at her school planner and drew a big red X through the square on her calendar that said Tuesday, September 3. That's today, she thought. Only thirty-eight days to go. Then she'd be back where she belonged.

At lunch she took her tattered bag out of her backpack and searched it inch by inch for plastic spiders, but she found only the tuna fish sandwich and fruit cup she'd put in the bag herself that morning.

Carrie and Sophie and Alex were eating together under a tree near the fence. Mark was there too. For a minute Lissa thought she might go over and sit with them. After all, hadn't Carrie asked her to walk home? And even though she hadn't liked Alex's joke, he had paid attention to her.

Maybe they were waiting for her to make a move.

She started in their direction. Her stomach joggled around like a basketball that someone had just slam-dunked down her throat.

When she grew up and had kids, she was never, ever going to move. She was never going to make her kids be the new kid.

In the school yard, the littler kids were skipping and playing hopscotch, but to Lissa they were a blur. All she could see were Carrie and Sophie trading sandwiches while Alex and Mark played with something that looked like a Game Boy. She was almost close enough to call out to them when Otis appeared at her side like a bumblebee. Even though the rain had stopped, he was still wearing his yellow slicker.

"I heard what those kids were saying about you," he said.

Lissa's heart stopped. She looked at Otis. His eyes widened behind their thick lenses. "Carrie said her mom made her ask you to walk home. She was only asking you to make her mom stop bugging her."

"How do you know?"

Otis looked embarrassed. "I just heard them, okay?"

"No, that's not okay, Otis. How do you know?"

"I listened."

"Listened? To who?"

"Whom."

"What?"

"Listened to whom."

Lissa groaned. Otis was going to drive her crazy.

"Whom is the right way of saying it because . . ."

"Okay! Okay! Okay! Whom!"

"Promise not to get mad?"

"No! I won't promise anything. Now tell me before I squash you!"

"I snuck up behind Carrie and Sophie when they were walking down the hall, and I heard Carrie say, 'You won't believe what I have to do. My mom is making me invite that new kid to my house today.'"

Lissa didn't want to believe it, but she knew it was true. Why else would Carrie suddenly suggest they walk home? She'd lived next door for over three weeks and Carrie had hardly even said hello.

Under the tree the four friends started to laugh. Even though Lissa knew it was dumb, she felt they were laughing at her.

Just imagine if she'd actually gone over there! Her face flushed.

The bell rang, and Lissa turned and ran toward the school. Otis trotted along behind her.

"I'll meet you at your locker when school's out. Okay, Lissa?"

Lissa felt like screaming, "Leave me alone," but Otis couldn't help that he was the most annoying little kid on the whole planet. And she'd accepted the job, so she had to be nice to him, even if she'd rather eat one of his pickled eyeballs.

So, she just turned to him and said, "I'll meet you at the corner behind the library. At 3:30. But don't tell anyone you're waiting for me. It'll be our secret."

Otis nodded seriously. "Just like spies, huh?"

"That's right. Like spies." And if I'm really lucky no one will see us together ever, thought Lissa.

Otis pushed his glasses up his nose and looked at Lissa. "I can't wait, Lissa. See you then!" He ran off, his yellow slicker dragging behind him.

"Boo!" said a voice behind her. Lissa jumped.

Carrie and Alex laughed. "Scare you?"

Lissa shook her head.

"Well if Otis doesn't scare you, nothing will," said Carrie. "He's a weirdo."

"Yeah," said Lissa. "What's with that yellow slicker, anyway?"

Another cloud passed over the sun. A few drops of rain started to fall.

"Well make sure he doesn't put a hex on you," said Alex.

"Since you two are together all the time," Carrie said with a hint of a sneer.

"I'm not his friend," said Lissa. "His dad's paying me to be nice to him."

"Really?" said Carrie. Lissa nodded.

"Well there isn't enough money in Harmony Beach to make me hang out with him," Carrie said, shaking her hair. "Come on, Alex." They ran toward the school.

Lissa looked around. She hoped no one had heard her tell Carrie that she wasn't Otis's friend. She hung her head and watched a tear fall on the damp ground. Darn that Otis, anyway!

Chapter Six

Otis was waiting behind the library just as she had instructed. He was clutching a half-eaten, wormy looking apple in one hand and holding a giant black umbrella in the other. The drizzle had started again, and Lissa stalked over to him and nodded curtly.

Otis jumped up happily when he saw her. Lissa said a little prayer of thanks that it was raining. All the kids had disappeared right after school. There was no one around to see her and Otis walk home.

"Hi, Lissa, want one?" Otis held out another shriveled and bruised apple.

"No thanks."

They walked in silence until they got to the corner of Oak Street.

Otis stopped at the corner. Lissa got to the giant tree on Otis's front lawn before she realized that he wasn't following her anymore. She turned. Why was he still at the corner?

"Come on!" she yelled.

Otis shook his head.

"What are you doing?"

Otis sat down on the stone wall. The giant umbrella stretched out over his head and shoulders like a bat wing.

Lissa walked back towards Otis.

"What are you sitting here for?"

"I'm not going home."

"Why not?"

"Because I want to show you my secret, and we have to go to the lake."

"Can't you show me tomorrow? When it's not raining?"

"No, I really want to show you today."

"Why is this secret so important, anyway?"

"Well, I've got to go to the lake whether you come or not," said Otis, hopping down from the wall and trudging off.

Lissa ran after him. "I guess I have to come then, don't I?"

"You don't have to even be my friend if you don't want to," he said.

For a moment Lissa wondered if Otis had heard what she'd said to Carrie and Alex. She looked at him carefully, but his eyes didn't give anything away. That little feeling of guilt squelched around in her stomach again. It wasn't a nice feeling, and it reminded Lissa of something her grandmother always used to tell her: "Never say or do anything you wouldn't want to see printed on the front page of the paper." When she thought about it, she really wouldn't want her remarks about Otis printed on the front page of the paper.

Otis was watching her expectantly.

"Are you coming or not?"

"Okay, okay, okay."

Otis smiled.

Lissa gave a small smile in return.

Bay Street led down a sloping hill toward Bayside Park, which was beside a marshy outcropping. The weeds grew so high they were taller than Lissa. In the dark dank afternoon, they crowded in over the path, heavy with raindrops and as thick as a tightly woven mat. Otis led the way, his determined little figure cutting a swathe through the dense brush. A giant blade of marsh grass slapped Lissa in the face. It was an obstacle course made up of mud, giant vines and overgrown insects.

"Just exactly where are we going, anyway?" she asked.

"It's not far now." Otis sounded excited. He turned, and Lissa almost bumped into him.

"My mom used to bring me here," he said. "We'd come down here and look at the birds. Over here," he pointed to a stone bridge that spanned a pond, "is where the carp spawn in the spring. And there," he swung around and gazed out on the lake, "is where the Canada geese come in by the hundreds. This bay used to be called Pigeon Bay because a hundred years ago so many passenger pigeons used to fly through here that they'd break the tree branches when they stopped to roost."

"Wow!" Lissa tried to imagine the surrounding trees thick with birds, their branches drooping to the ground, the air pulsing with their cooing call and fluttering wings. "That would have been something to see."

"Passenger pigeons are extinct now. People shot them all because they were a nuisance. Some people say the last of the species was shot right here on this beach."

"You sure know a lot about nature," Lissa said, impressed in spite of herself.

"Well, like I said. My mom was a biologist. And she was also part Native. She taught me all kinds of stuff about different Native beliefs. She said her grandfather used to tell her that there are many ways to the High Place and that the things one tribe believes can help another understand its own beliefs better. Lots of native people believe there are spirits in everything around us, though. Even animals and plants."

"That's cool, Otis," said Lissa.

"Yeah, her great grandmother was Ojibway. That makes me part Ojibway too," Otis pointed out seriously.

"Is that your secret, Otis?"

"That's part of it, but my secret is much, much better than all this stuff combined."

Lissa followed Otis through the dense

growth to the shore. The lake stretched out before them, dark and gloomy, and full of eddying currents. The sun was completely hidden by the steady drizzle. Lissa shivered. Seagulls squealed and wheeled in the soggy sky. A lonely duck floated by; there was a strange rustling on the riverbank, and a pair of kingfishers scolded noisily from a branch of the giant chestnut tree. The lake smelled a little like dead fish, and algae lined the shore. Lissa wondered how far they were going when Otis stopped in front of an old rundown boathouse.

"Who does this belong to?" asked Lissa.

"Old man Gordon who lives in town. He never comes out here anymore. No one comes here but me."

The water lapped hollowly against the pilings holding the dock in place. Lissa could see a hole in the roof and a battered old canoe turned on its side.

Otis turned and looked at Lissa. "Before we go any farther, you have to promise me not to tell anyone about this. You have to swear by your guardian spirit."

"What's that mean?"

"My mom believed that each person had a guardian spirit."

"Kind of like a guardian angel?" Lissa thought that this was an interesting idea. "Your mom must have been a really amazing person." She reached over and patted Otis's arm. Sometimes her mom made her really mad — like when she'd dragged her all the way across the country to live in a place where nobody liked her — but at least she had a mom. She remembered her mom stroking her forehead last night.

"Don't you have any grandparents?"

"Yeah. My mom's father lives on Manitoulin Island. He visits us sometimes."

"What about your dad's parents?"

Otis was silent for a moment. "My grandmother lives in Maine. My grandfather died five years ago. I don't remember him really."

"Do you ever see your grandmother?"

"Sometimes. My dad's father was the one who gave us all those stuffed animals." Otis stopped. He studied her. "You never answered me."

Lissa was confused. Then she remembered. Otis had asked her to swear by her guardian spirit. Since she didn't really believe in guardian spirits, she guessed it would be all right if she swore by hers, whatever it was. Lissa didn't want to promise to keep any kind of secret, but the rain was coming down harder than ever and a cold wind was beginning to make the waves crash against the pilings. The rickety old dock creaked underfoot, and all at once all Lissa wanted to do was get home to a hot drink and some dry clothes. Now she could understand why Otis wore that yellow slicker. Even on a good day the marsh, the damp and the mud would be icky.

"Do you promise?" Otis's googly eyes hypnotized her.

"Oh, all right. I swear by my guardian spirit . . . whatever that is," she added, just so Otis would know she wasn't really buying into all this spirit stuff.

"Now cross your heart and hope to die," Otis finished.

"Cross my heart and hope to . . . What for?" Lissa demanded.

"I just like to cover all the bases," Otis said solemnly.

Lissa shivered. "Cross my heart and hope to die," she said between chattering teeth.

"Okay, come on, then."

Otis took her hand and led her into the boathouse. Inside it was even more rickety and dank smelling. Underfoot, through the slatted boards, the lake licked greedily at her feet. Rain poured through the hole in the roof. It was very dark.

"Over here," Otis had moved away and crouched in a corner, his yellow slicker surrounding his small body.

Lissa felt her way toward him with her toe.

A loud screech stopped her in her tracks.

A big bird was hunched in a wire cage in the corner of the boathouse.

"My gosh, Otis, that looks like a hawk."

Otis looked up; his eyes were shining. "It is. It's a red tailed hawk. That's where I got this feather." He held up his special feather.

"What's it doing here?"

"I'm keeping it safe." Otis pulled a piece of fish out of his backpack and fed it to the bird.

"Where did it come from?" Lissa watched, fascinated, as the bird held the fish with its talons and ripped away chunks with its sharp beak.

"That's the other part of the secret," said Otis, glancing around as if someone might be listening.

"You mean there's more?"

Otis sat down and crossed his legs. He gestured for Lissa to do the same. "Like I told you, my mom believed that there are spirits in everything. I think that when my mom got to the spirit world she went to the Creator, offered tobacco, and asked Him to send the hawk to tell me she was still with me."

Lissa stared at him as if he'd gone completely crazy. But he seemed the same serious bug-eyed Otis. Rain dripped off his hat onto the floor. Lissa stared at the fierce looking bird. Its eyes were shiny and dark like blackberries. It seemed to be waiting for her reaction. Lissa gulped. She really wanted to go home.

"You don't believe me, do you?"

"No, Otis, I don't." Fear made Lissa angry. "It's just a dumb old bird, for Pete's sake."

Otis didn't look upset. "No, it's not. There's a story my mom's grandfather told her about how Original Man's grandmother,

Nokomis, was sent to live with the moon and watch over all the women on the earth. I bet my mom thought I should have someone to watch over me, so she asked the Creator to send me a spirit." He nodded at the hawk. "That spirit is Scarlett. I know it."

Lissa sat down heavily on the boards. "You know, Otis. I really miss my friends in Victoria, and I miss my dad. I know how bad I feel when I think about all the people back home. So you must really miss your mom, huh?"

"I've got Scarlett to keep me company now, though," Otis said.

"But Otis, how can you believe this bird is sent by the Creator?"

"The day my mom disappeared Scarlett was in the tree fort. I found her when I went up there to hide from mean old Alex. He always chased me, ever since I was three. No one ever went up in that tree fort but my mom and me. Scarlett was there, even though I'd never seen a hawk in that tree before." For a minute Lissa thought he might start to cry. But he cleared his throat and continued, "She wouldn't go away. When she almost got eaten by Mrs. Martin's cat, she let me put her in that old wire bird cage. I brought her here on my wagon. Then my dad came home from searching for my mom in B.C. and told me it looked like my mom was dead. I was really really sad, until I figured it out: My mom asked the Creator to send Scarlett to watch out for me."

"She's a wild hawk, though, Otis. You're going to have to let her go one day."

"She won't go. I know she won't. She's here to watch over me. Why else would she have come the day my mom disappeared?"

"Don't you know what a coincidence is? And suppose something happens? Suppose someone finds her?"

"No one has found her yet."

"Otis, I really think you should tell your dad about this."

"My dad doesn't like to talk about my mom. I don't think he'd want to talk about this."

"So, why did you tell me?"

"You're like me."

"What do you mean?"

"You don't have any friends. Just like me. I thought we could be friends."

Lissa stood up. "Otis, I'm three whole years older than you. I just moved here. I'm going to make friends one of these days. I'm nothing like you."

Otis stood up. "Don't you want to be my friend?"

"Sure, but . . ."

Outside, the wind howled. Scarlett flapped her wings and screeched.

Otis said, "Time to go."

"I just don't think it's right to keep her cooped up in here, Otis. Even if you're right about spirit guides and all . . . " What the heck am I saying, Lissa wondered. Even if he's *right?* I must be as nuts as he is.

The day had darkened even further. Heavy clouds hung from the sky like possums. When they got back to Otis's, Baskerville sniffed them over energetically, inhaling the smell of the lake, the weeds and the bird.

A yellow light burned in the room over the garage. "Your dad's still working," said Lissa as they hung up their coats in the mud-room.

"I told you, he's always working." Otis seemed quieter than usual. Lissa hoped she hadn't made him sorry about telling her his secret. But she was worried. She'd sworn on her spirit guide *and* crossed her heart and hoped to die. That had to count for something.

"Come on in here, Lissa," said Otis after he'd taken off his giant yellow slicker and hung it on a nail in the back hallway. "I want to show you something." He led Lissa up the stairs to his room, flattened himself on his stomach and rummaged around under his bed. The first thing he pulled out was a rubber snake, followed by a box of Lego. Finally, he pulled out a small, dusty looking book. "Here it is," he said in a hushed voice. "The book."

Lissa stared at the cover. It was a book about Ojibway beliefs. Otis was very solemn as he opened to a chapter on religious and ceremonial life. "I got this from my mom's bookshelf. Look." He pointed at a picture of a young boy sitting on a rock. "It says here that sometimes young boys go on something called a vision quest."

"Vision quest?" asked Lissa.

"Yeah, it was to receive the blessing of a spirit that would help and protect him in his life. See, it says so right here."

Lissa took the book from Otis and read the paragraph he was pointing to. "It says here you have to go into the woods alone and fast for several days!" She looked up in alarm. "Promise me you won't try anything like that."

Otis took the book back and closed it. He didn't answer her.

Lissa couldn't think of anything to say. Otis seemed so sure. She couldn't see the harm in letting him believe the hawk was a spirit sent by his mother. Nothing bad could come of that, surely. But she'd have to convince him to let the hawk go. He couldn't keep going down to the lake day after day, especially with the cold and rainy season coming. And there was another thing. Out on the lake she'd seen crazy wooden structures spring up overnight. Her mother had told her they were duck blinds and that hunters used them to hide from ducks. The lake wasn't a very safe place for Otis to be right now, and the bird would be sure to be spooked by the gunshots.

All these things somersaulted through Lissa's mind as she sat in Otis's room, pondering his question. A door slammed at the back of the house, followed by a couple of deep, rumbly woofs from Baskerville.

"That's my dad," said Otis.

"Otis. Lissa," shouted Mr. Striker. "Come on down. I've got something to tell you."

Otis shoved the book under his bed. Lissa was going to say something, but Otis vanished down the stairs. Slowly Lissa followed.

Mr. Striker was standing at the bottom of the back staircase. He smiled when Otis came clattering towards him. "Hi, you two. Have a good afternoon?"

Otis said, "Yeah, Dad. I showed Lissa around town." He shot Lissa a warning look.

Cross my heart and hope to die, thought Lissa. Boy, am I dumb.

"Well, I've got to go to Collingwood on Saturday to do a little research. I thought you could stay at Lissa's."

"I'd rather come with you, Dad." Otis said, his eyes on the floor.

"Not this time, Otis. I'm going to be crawling in and out of caves. Not the safest place for a kid. You don't mind if Otis stays at your house, do you Lissa?"

"Well," Lissa desperately tried to think of what to say. Otis looked so sad. She wished his dad would see that Otis was saying one thing and thinking another. "I'll have to ask my mom," was all she could come up with.

"I've already phoned her," said Mr. Striker. "She said it was fine with her."

Lissa looked at Otis. His bony shoulders slumped. He bent his head and fondled Baskerville's ears. Baskerville thumped his tail happily.

"Isn't that great Lissa? I can come for sure," Otis said in a small voice. He kept his eyes on Baskerville who put his face on Otis's knee and licked his fingers.

"Uh, I guess so . . . "

Mr. Striker had gone into his study. "That's that then. I'll be leaving first thing Saturday morning," he said over his shoulder as he moved deeper into the room. "Better pack some warm clothes. Weather forecast is for cold and rain."

Lissa put on her coat. Otis had already thrown his magician's cape over his shoulders. He tapped a black magician's wand against his sleeve and pulled out a giant flower. "See, Lissa, I believe in magic."

"Bye, Otis." It was already getting dark by the time Lissa headed down the stone walk. Otis watched her from the window, waving the giant flower at her.

Chapter Seven

"Lissa, time to rise and shine." Bill flicked the overhead light in Lissa's room.

Lissa moaned and burrowed deeper under the covers. If only she could spend the rest of her life in bed. She just had too many things to think about these days. At least it was Friday and both her first week of school and first week of looking after Otis were almost over. A gust of wind set the tree branches outside her window to tapping on the glass, and Muggsy whimpered anxiously as if expecting another thunderstorm.

"I know just how you feel, Muggsy,"

.c from under the covers.

Lissa!" Mom came to the door. "Hurry
. I made pancakes."

"Coming," Lissa grunted.

Attracted by the smell of breakfast,
Muggsy followed Lissa's mom out of the
room.

"Traitor," Lissa called after him.

When she came down to breakfast, Bill
looked up from his paper. "Hey, Liss. How
were your first three days on the job?"

"Okay." For a minute Lissa considered
telling her mom and Bill about the lake and
the bird and the strange feeling she had about
Otis and his interest in magic and spirits. Although she'd promised to keep his secret, she
was worried about Otis and what he was up
to. She was tired of going to the lake every
day. Otis hadn't really done anything wrong,
but she had to convince him to do something
about the hawk. And soon.

"Want a drive to school, Lissa?" asked
Bill. He took a sip of coffee. "I'm going to be
driving right by there in about five minutes."

"Okay," said Lissa, mopping up syrup
with the last of her pancakes. "Remember
that permission slip you signed? We're go-

ing on a beach clean up to Point Pelee today."

"Rotten weather for it," said Bill, standing up and stretching.

"Bundle up, hon," said Mom.

The buses were waiting when Bill pulled
into the driveway, their engines idling. In class
Ms. Johnson was directing the students to
remember their lunches and handing out la-
tex gloves and plastic garbage bags.

Sophie and Carrie and Alex were standing together, laughing and looking in Lissa's
direction. She turned her head and tried to
ignore them. When they all trooped on the
bus, Lissa pretended not to notice where the
others were sitting. The rain had spattered
her glasses and she swiped at the drops with
the back of her hand. Someone sat down beside her, and she looked up into the face of
Ms. Johnson.

"Well, Lissa. How are you liking Harmony Beach?"

Why were people always asking her how
she liked something? It made it difficult to
tell the truth. They only wanted her to say
what they wanted to hear anyway. Even her
mom didn't want to hear that she hated it

here. When Lissa didn't answer, Ms. Johnson said, "Oh, I see. You don't feel at home here yet, do you?"

Lissa shook her head. Her eyes flooded and Ms. Johnson blurred into a shapeless form.

"Give it a little time, Lissa. You can't rush how you feel."

Ms. Johnson started talking about the history of Point Pelee and the types of wildlife that were found there. Lissa stared ahead, grateful that she didn't have to answer any more questions. In the back of the bus, Carrie and Sophie squealed with laughter. Another yell rang out and Ms. Johnson got up to see what was going on.

Lissa stared straight ahead until she felt someone tapping her on the shoulder. The drawstrings in her throat had loosened just a little so she muttered, "What?"

"Want to be my partner for the beach clean up?" said a voice. Lissa looked over her shoulder. It was the tall thin girl she had seen around the school yard, picking up other people's lunch garbage. Lissa had also seen her helping the kindergarten kids across the street. Carrie had called her a hippy-dippy freakazoid. She had braces and straight black hair that was cut short and spiky.

"My name's Julie," she said as she moved forward. "Is it okay if I sit here?"

Lissa nodded. Julie plunked herself down and smiled, revealing a mouth full of metal. "I've always wanted to go to B.C. Have you ever seen a whale in the wild?"

"All the time," Lissa answered. "On the ferry from Swartz Bay to Tsawwassen, I've seen pods of orcas."

"Wow!" Julie said. "That must be so amazing. My family is planning a trip out there next summer and I'm dying to see a whale."

"There are boats that take you whale watching," said Lissa. "But I've seen them in the water just off Beach Drive in Victoria. And seals too. You can feed wild seals at the marina."

"Maybe you can come over one day," said Julie. "My mom would like to meet you. She was born in Victoria."

"Maybe my mom knows her," Lissa said.

"Do you think so?" Julie asked, pleased at the idea.

Ms. Johnson lurched up beside them as

the bus made a turn into the parking lot at the Point. "Don't worry, Julie," she said as Julie started to get up. "I'll just sit back here." She sank into Julie's empty seat. "Those kids need to burn off some energy."

In spite of the weather, the day turned out to be fun. Lissa and Julie got an award for filling the most garbage bags with trash and even Carrie couldn't spoil Lissa's fun — not even when she muttered, "Losers" in a stage whisper as Ms. Johnson handed each girl a book called *The Importance of Preserving Canada's Wetlands*.

It wasn't until Lissa remembered that she had to walk home with Otis that her mood darkened. Sure enough, when the bus pulled into the school driveway, there he was, his yellow slicker glowing like an amber traffic light. Today he was carrying a giant gnarled walking stick, which he waved excitedly at the bus after he saw Lissa's face in the window.

"Is that kid waving at you?" asked Julie, pointing at Otis.

"Yeah," Lissa began.

"Hey, Lissa, your boyfriend's blowing kisses," shouted Alex from the back of the bus. Everyone laughed and Lissa slumped down in her seat. Julie looked at all the laughing faces and turned back to Lissa.

"Do you know who that is?"

"Yeah," said Lissa. "He lives across the street from me."

"I mean," said Julie. "Do you know who he *is*?"

"What do you mean?"

"He's a poor little kid who's always pretending to put spells on people. He walks around with a stick he calls a magic wand. The little kids are scared of him and the big kids think he's nuts. And his dad writes these really creepy horror books about vampires and monsters."

Otis was hopping up and down now, waving his walking stick. A teacher came over and put his hand on Otis's shoulder. He pointed to his eye and Lissa knew he was telling Otis that he might poke somebody's eye out.

Lissa sighed. She might as well get it over with. "His dad asked me to sort of watch him after school. He's waiting for me to walk home with him."

"Lissa, you better not keep the alien waiting," said Sophie as she and Carrie pushed down the bus steps.

Carrie made a face at Otis as she walked by, and he stared back at her. He made an arc with his hands and pretended to toss some kind of imaginary ball at her back. Carrie stumbled and turned around, her face puzzled.

"There! Did you see that?" asked Julie.

"Don't be silly," said Lissa, pointing at an empty Tetra Pak box that had blown into the gutter. "Carrie just snubbed her toe on that juice box."

"Okay, if you say so." Julie said. "So do you really go into his house? You know his mom disappeared."

"His mom was a biologist who disappeared on a trip in the Rocky Mountains. She was swept away by an avalanche. Don't be silly, Julie."

Julie didn't look hurt. Instead, she looked impressed. "Boy, you're really brave. I don't think I'd want to spend any time in that house. My brother used to deliver papers there and he told me they've got dead animals all over the place. He said they're going to stuff that giant dog of theirs when he dies."

Lissa picked up her backpack. She was beginning to feel a little sorry for Otis. If even the nice kids like Julie felt that way about him, no wonder he was having trouble making friends. It was just like moving, only worse, she decided. After all, Otis had lived in Harmony Beach his entire life.

"Hey, Otis," she said when she hopped off the bottom step onto the damp gravel. "Ready to go?"

Julie jumped down behind her. "Can I walk with you too? I live two blocks away from you and Otis."

Otis looked at Julie and nodded.

"Okay," Lissa said.

Julie hoisted her backpack onto her shoulder. "Look, Otis," she said, "Lissa and I got a prize for being the best garbage collectors." She showed him the book on wetlands.

Even though Otis's eyes looked distorted behind his thick lenses, Lissa was sure they lit up when Julie held out the book.

"Yeah, Otis," she said. "I got one too. Maybe we can look at it when we get to your house."

Otis raised his stick like a drum major. "Onward," he said.

The three of them — short yellow Otis, medium frizzy-haired Lissa and tall spiky-haired Julie — headed across the school yard.

When they got to Julie's corner, Julie

waved as she walked away. "Maybe one day you can come to my house after school. I'll ask my mom," she called back over her shoulder.

Otis looked at Lissa as if to ask if he'd be going too.

"Yeah, Otis," said Julie. "You too. My mom really likes your dad's books. Maybe he can autograph one for her."

Otis smiled — a rare sight, Lissa realized. Her heart lightened.

After Julie waved good-bye and headed across the park toward her house, Otis and Lissa went on toward Linden Street. At the corner, Otis turned south, towards the lake.

Lissa sighed. With all the good things that had happened that day, she had almost forgotten about the hawk.

"Otis, I have to talk to you about Scarlett," she said.

Otis marched on.

"I don't think you can keep that bird in the boathouse much longer. Hunting season's starting soon. It's not safe."

"It's not a bird. It's a spirit sent by my mother," Otis said.

"I think you should tell someone about this. I really do," Lissa pleaded.

"No!"

"Otis, you've got to."

"No!" He turned and looked at Lissa. "And you can't either. You promised."

"I know, I know, but listen for a minute."

"No!" said Otis and he took off at a run.

Lissa watched him go, his short legs under the billowing slicker churning through the puddles like a pair of paddle wheels.

"Otis, wait!" she screamed after him. He was going in a different direction from usual, heading for the entrance to the park that was bordered by the heaviest part of the marsh. Lissa had never gone that way before. Some of the kids at school told stories about marsh monsters and ghosts of children who had wandered away and never been seen again.

What have I gotten myself into? she thought, tempted to let him go on alone.

But she had no choice. She'd promised to look out for him.

Reluctantly, Lissa followed Otis into the marsh and through the wet clinging grass toward the fog-choked beach.

Chapter Eight

Lissa looked wildly around her. Otis had disappeared into the fog, thick as bonfire smoke. She caught sight of his rain slicker and breathed a sigh of relief. He was over to her left, moving in the direction of the boathouse, or at least in the direction she remembered the boathouse to be.

Lissa picked her way along the beach, stepping over the dead fish and other debris that had washed up in the night. Every so often she'd glimpse Otis's slicker, a little flame of yellow, in the ash-colored fog. He knew his way around better than she, but even so, Lissa was worried.

He'd been so upset when she'd said he should let the hawk go. She hoped he'd watch where he was going. What's more, she hoped she'd be able to remember where *she* was going. She'd only been to the boathouse three times and never along this particular path. The rain and fog were making the overgrown path even harder to follow.

"Otis, wait!" she yelled. "I won't tell anyone. I promise!"

No answer.

She trudged on, slapping the thistles aside with the sleeve of her jacket. Water gurgled around her ankles. She'd stepped into the creek, which, after all the rain, was deep and fast moving. She knew she wouldn't be able to cross it without getting swept away. Tears stung the back of her eyes.

A sudden cracking noise made her jump. Duck hunters. Someone was out on the lake even though hunting season hadn't officially started. Lissa crouched down and held her breath. More distant popping noise, like firecrackers. The fog muffled them, but Lissa could still tell that they were coming from the direction of the boathouse.

Lissa's heart pounded wildly. She turned

away from the lake and began to slash through the long grass along the bank of the creek. If she followed the creek she would end up at the stone bridge that crossed the creek and led into the park, and from there, she could go down the familiar path to the boathouse. The water in the creek, which had been slow and sleepy in the summer, had swelled in all the rain to a rushing stream. A broken branch eddied down the current, snagged on a rock, then, flushed by the force of the water, shot into the lake. At the bend, a sleek furry creature scurried along the edge and slipped quickly into the water, its brown head slick and wet and suddenly black in the turbulent water. It dove under and disappeared, leaving only a trail of white bubbles behind it.

Lissa's boots were shiny with mud, her hair was plastered against her skull and it seemed farther to the bridge than she remembered. She stopped and forced herself to think. Precious seconds were passing and her fear for Otis made her heart thud. If she didn't find the bridge soon, she would have to try to wade across the rushing water. On an impulse, she turned around and headed back towards the lake, hoping that she'd find a place where the stream narrowed. The weeds on the creek bank squelched underfoot as she retraced her steps.

Lissa couldn't search for a good crossing spot any longer. She was going to have to wade through the water. She rolled up her pants and took one tentative step. The water was up to the middle of her shin. She took another step. Then another. Pieces of debris, bits of wood and fallen leaves, swirled around her knees and she stumbled, soaking herself up to her neck and swallowing a mouthful of earthy tasting water.

She reached the other side, grabbed the root of an exposed tree and hauled herself onto the muddy bank. She almost cried with relief. Now, the boathouse. Summoning up her best memory of the where the boathouse was located, she began slicing her way through the long grass. Every so often a gunshot made her jump. The further she went, the heavier the weeds became. It seemed like hours since she'd last caught sight of Otis. She forced herself not to think of all the things that might have happened to him.

"Otis!" she yelled as loudly as she could.

At first, no answer, just the crashing of

the waves along the rocks and the wind lashing through the trees. Then, a faint cry, almost an echo, muted by the wind.

"Lissa, help!"

Lissa strained to hear which direction the voice was coming from, but the wind was dancing about, muffling the sounds, tossing them in all directions.

She kept walking. Every few steps she stopped, called out, "Otis!" and listened.

Worried as she was about Otis, she almost missed the roof of the boathouse as it loomed out of the mist. Thank heavens, she thought. At least, she had come the right way. She had her mouth open to shout again when she heard a weak little yell.

"Lissa!" called a voice. "Lissa?"

It sounded like Otis and it sounded like he was losing strength. Panic-stricken, she looked around her. The boathouse broke through the mist, then disappeared. She squinted. "Is somebody there?"

"Lissa, it's me! Otis!"

"Otis!" cried Lissa as relief made her weak. "Where are you?"

"Over here. I'm in the water. Hurry!"

Lissa's fear grew as she crashed her way

along the path and down the dock to the boat-house. A huge hole in the rickety dock opened up under her. She heard the voice again — this time it came from the hole. "I'm here, Lissa. Down here."

Lissa fell to her knees and peered into the roiling water. Through the hole in the planks, she could just make out Otis's bedraggled form, clinging to a piling, his hat floating behind him, his yellow slicker and sodden clothes dragging him down with each crash of the waves.

"Hang on, Otis, I'm coming!" yelled Lissa as she looked around for something to throw to him. She had to get him out of there and she had to do it soon.

She ran back to the shore. All she could do was wade in and pull him out. She stripped off her wet and soggy outer clothes.

"Otis, can you take off that raincoat?" she yelled through the screeching wind, as she started into the water.

"I can't let go of the dock," he screamed back.

The water licked hungrily at her legs as she forced herself forward against the wind.

As she got closer, the bottom of the lake

dipped sharply, plunging Lissa in over her head. She came up gasping and swam onward, thankful for all the swimming lessons her mom had signed her up for. When she got to Otis, she helped him hold onto the dock.

"Now," she said. "Get rid of all those heavy clothes or they'll drag you under."

She grabbed Otis around the waist as he struggled out of his coat. Under the water he kicked off his shoes. The water jumped madly around them, splashing into their noses, and in great gulping waves down their throats.

Otis coughed and sputtered. "I'm scared, Lissa."

Somehow, Lissa forced herself to remain calm. "I'm going to have to tow you in, Otis. Can you swim?"

Otis nodded. "A little."

Hanging on to the piling with one arm, and Otis with the other, she commanded, "Turn on your back. Remember to stay calm. Kick a little if you can and don't worry, I've got you."

The shore was fifty yards away, but the deep water only lasted for fifty feet. I can do this, Lissa said to herself. I can do this. She hooked her arm across Otis's bony chest, grasped him under his arm, let go of the piling, and started swimming. The waves crashed over her head. Behind her, Otis kicked and flailed, but stayed afloat. Lissa's toes hit the sandy bottom in minutes.

She pulled Otis forward until his feet were steady on the ground. Together, they staggered out of the water. Otis had lost his glasses. Both were coughing and out of breath.

Otis was sobbing.

"She's gone."

It took Lissa a moment to understand what Otis was saying.

"You mean Scarlett's gone."

Otis's whole body was shaking. "I, I, I went into the boathouse. It was so dark, I c-c-c-couldn't see. Then I s-s-saw that the cage was broken. She's not there. I think someone may have hurt her. I was so worried I forgot about the hole in the dock, and on the way out, I fell into the water." He hiccuped and coughed.

Lissa put her arm around Otis's shoulders. Again, she was surprised at how thin and bony they were. He was always covered up with capes and raincoats, Lissa realized.

He was always wearing a costume.

"You might have drowned!"

Lissa looked him over carefully. He had a cut on his knee and a bump on his forehead, over his left eye. He was shivering violently. Lissa said a silent prayer of thanks that he hadn't knocked himself out when he landed in the water and that she'd arrived in time.

"I bet the duck hunters let her go. I think they used the boathouse as a duck blind." He tried to choke it back, but a giant sob escaped.

"I'm so sorry, Otis. But maybe it's for the best. You didn't see any sign that she was hurt, did you? She was just gone?"

He nodded.

"Then she escaped somehow. She's off flying south. Do hawks fly south, Otis?"

He sobbed again. "I, I, I don't know."

"I bet they do. I bet she's hooking up with other hawks and going south. What do you think?"

"I want to know for s-s-sure she escaped. I want to know she's okay."

"Let's come back tomorrow, Otis, and look at the boathouse and see if we can figure it out." Lissa shivered. The wind was picking up. "Look at us, we're both soaked.

And it's dark and foggy. We'll come back tomorrow and look around. Okay?"

Otis stopped sobbing. "What if she's hurt now?"

"You didn't see any signs of that, did you?"

He shook his head.

"Then I'm sure everything's all right. Come on, Otis. Let's go home."

Reluctantly, he let Lissa lead him through the undergrowth. The path, so hard to find before, opened up in front of her along with the bridge, the weeping willow and the brick stairs that led toward the pavilion.

Otis stopped crying, but was shivering even harder. Lissa didn't know much about shock, but she knew she'd have to get him warm soon.

"Come on, Otis. We're almost there."

No answer.

Lissa hoped her mom was home. Otis hadn't spoken for twenty minutes. He'd just shuffled along, his teeth chattering, his eyes glazed over.

In her book, *The Secret in the Belfry*, the main character had suffered from shock when a snake had bitten her. From what Lissa remembered of shock, it usually followed a bad injury of some kind. They passed no one on the way across the park. The heavy fog patches were intermittent but as thick and clinging as a spider's web. Most people were snug and cozy in their houses, but at the park entrance a man was out walking his dog. When he caught sight of the two bedraggled shapes struggling through the long grass, he shouted, "Are you two kids all right?"

Lissa recognized the man as Mr. McGregor, the groundskeeper. She'd seen him in the summer, working the gardens, and he'd been one of the only people who'd welcomed her to Harmony Beach. "Otis fell in the water," she said.

"Well, you two better come with me. I'll get you warmed up in a flash. And we better call your parents."

Otis was shivering so hard that he could barely walk. Mr. McGregor handed Lissa the leash, hoisted Otis onto his back and set off across the park. Mr. McGregor lived in a tiny, old wooden house that at one time had been a summer cottage. Inside, a fire glowed in the grate and two small yellow lights bathed the tiny kitchen in comforting warmth.

"Here you go, laddie. Sit right here and have a nice cup of tea." Mr. McGregor busied himself at the stove. "As for you, lassie, there are some dry clothes in there," he pointed to a large cupboard. "My grandchildren leave something here every time they visit. Why don't you see what fits?" He tossed a giant towel to Otis. "Let's get you dried off and see if you've shrunk any." He rubbed Otis's back briskly. "Hand me some dry things for the lad here while you're at it," he called to Lissa.

Lissa rummaged through the sweatshirts, jeans, old socks and t-shirts until she found a pair of gray sweatpants and a hooded navy sweatshirt, which she tossed to Mr. McGregor. For herself, she discovered a pair of ripped corduroy pants, black sweat socks and a fuzzy purple wool sweater. Gradually Otis's teeth had stopped clattering.

The kettle sent up a piercing whistle, and Mr. McGregor handed Otis the towel and told him to dry his hair. He crossed over to the stove and filled a big brown teapot with steaming water and covered it with a tea cozy in the shape of a boat.

Flossie, Mr. McGregor's border collie,

wandered around the room, sniffing at the discarded wet clothing and whining with each gust of wind, as if she were scolding the two of them for taking such risks in foul weather.

In the safe small room, Otis's fall, her panic and her daring swim through the angry waters began to seem like a dream.

Mr. McGregor's voice pulled her back. "I think one of you had better phone your parents."

Lissa spoke first, "I'll see if my mom's home. She's a nurse, but I don't think she was working today."

Mr. McGregor nodded. "Good idea. Just what the laddie here needs, a good going over by a professional."

Lissa almost burst into tears when she heard her mother's voice on the phone.

"Mom, I'm at Mr. McGregor's, the groundskeeper in the park. Yes, Otis is here too. That's why I'm calling. You better come and pick us up. Otis fell in the lake and . . . "

Lissa's mom was on the front porch almost before Lissa had hung up the phone. Lissa had never been so happy to see anyone in her whole life.

Quickly she told her mom what had happened. Mr. McGregor pulled Lissa's mom aside. "I couldn't find anything wrong with the laddie," he said quietly, "but he looks mighty pale." They talked together in low voices while Lissa sat on the arm of Otis's chair.

"Don't tell them about Scarlett, Lissa. Please!" Otis whispered.

"Why not?"

"They'll think I'm crazy, and besides, she's gone so there's no reason to tell them."

"How are we going to explain why we were down here at the lake in this awful weather?" Otis looked thoughtful for a minute. Then he said, "Let's say I was doing a science project on Canada geese and I came down to do research."

"In this weather?" Lissa hissed. "Otis, I'm not covering up for you on this." Before she could say more, her mom came over and knelt down in front of Otis.

"Okay, Otis, how about you answer some questions for me? Do you feel like you want to throw up?"

Otis shook his head. Lissa's mom nodded approvingly.

"How about dizzy? Are you dizzy?"

Otis shook his head.

Lissa's mom put her hand on Otis's forehead and sighed with relief. "No fever."

As she took his pulse, a little smile tugged at her lips.

"All systems go, big guy." She looked over at Lissa who had been holding her breath. Then she settled herself in a big comfy chair on the other side of the old cast iron stove. "Suppose you tell me how all this happened," she said, her voice firm.

Lissa wasn't sure what to say. She snuck a glance at Otis, hoping he'd tell her mom about the boathouse, the hawk and the duck hunters, but he just sat quietly, scratching Flossie's ears. His eyes without his glasses looked naked and sad.

She didn't want to lie. She wasn't going to lie; the situation was much too serious. Desperately she looked at Otis, willing him to speak up, but he stared at the floor.

Lissa was either going to have to lie to her mother or break her promise to Otis.

Otis kept staring at the floor, his jaw clenched. Her mother was waiting.

Lissa made her decision.

Chapter Nine

"He had a project," Lissa said. In the old chair, Otis's bony shoulders slumped under the old plaid blanket.

Lissa's mom stared at her carefully.

"What kind of project?"

"You tell her, Otis," Lissa said. It was the least he could do. Besides, he had the imagination to figure it out.

"A project about the migration patterns of Canada geese," Otis said solemnly.

Lissa blinked.

"It's due on Monday," he added.

Lissa's mom looked uncertain, but all she

said was, "Well, thank goodness nothing really bad happened. You better not come to the park again in weather like this, no matter what the reason. Is that clear?"

Otis and Lissa nodded at the same time.

In her heart, Lissa breathed a huge sigh of relief. It was all going to blow over, and she was going to get another chance to convince Otis that he needed to tell everybody the truth himself. And he wasn't going to have to keep coming to the lake every day now that the hawk was gone. She promised herself to keep a close eye on him. At the first sign of trouble, she was going to go straight to her mother and tell her everything.

Lissa sensed she was being watched and looked up. Her mom was studying her carefully.

Perhaps her mom didn't believe Otis after all. Lissa gulped. She had a feeling that her mother was going to have a lot more questions for her once she got home.

"Well, gang," her mom said. "Let's get going. I can't thank you enough for your help," she said to Mr. McGregor as she picked up Lissa's and Otis's wet clothes. "I don't like to think about what might have happened if they hadn't run into you."

"Oh, I didn't do very much," Mr. McGregor said. "The lassie here had things under control. She saved the laddie from drowning." He ruffled Lissa's red curls. "You're a right brave lassie. A real heroine."

Lissa blushed. Mom looked at her. "I guess that's true, Liss," she said. "Saving Otis was a brave thing to do." She put her arm around Otis. "You know what the Chinese say about that, don't you, Otis?"

He shook his head.

"Once you've saved a person's life, you're responsible for that person forever."

Otis smiled. "That's neat," he said. "You mean Lissa has to look out for me forever? Even after my dad stops paying her?"

"That's right," said Lissa's mom with a big smile while Lissa felt a tickle of guilt. "Now how about you two get yourselves into the car? I need to put all these wet things in a plastic bag." She followed Mr. McGregor out onto the glassed-in back porch.

Otis and Lissa scrambled through the blowing leaves and slanting rain and tumbled into the car. Otis huddled into the blanket. "Thanks, Lissa," he said.

Lissa squinted at him through the gloom. "I almost told her, Otis. I only didn't because we have to talk first."

Otis stared straight ahead.

Lissa continued, "You have to promise me that you'll never, never, run off like that again."

Otis didn't answer.

"Promise me Otis, or I'll have to break my promise."

"You can't!"

"Yes, I can. You made me promise not to tell anyone about Scarlett. And I've kept my promise so far. But I didn't promise not to tell why you're running around in a hurricane and falling into the lake. And if that means I have to tell about Scarlett and your spirit guide and all that, I will."

Otis squirmed in his seat. Lissa continued, "So, you have to swear that you won't try and go off again by yourself, especially while I'm looking after you."

Otis seemed to think this over. "Okay, I guess," he said.

Before Lissa could say anything else her mom jogged across the soggy grass, holding a plastic bag over her head. "Whew, that's a gale force wind out there." She turned the key in the ignition and backed down the long, root-wrinkled driveway. Slowly, she turned the car around and started down the darkened streets. "Looks like the power's gone out." The lights of the car sent a weak beam onto the trees and bushes, creating crazy shadows. The streets were almost empty. Every so often they'd pass another car, the lights sweeping over them like a searchlight.

Finally Mom pulled into Otis's driveway.

As if he'd sensed them coming, Baskerville was standing on his hind legs, his giant paws on the living room windowsill, watching for them like a huge dark ghost.

Lissa peered through the gloom and was upset to see that Mr. Striker's car wasn't in the driveway.

"Did your dad say he was going somewhere today?" Lissa's mom asked as they let themselves in the back door. Baskerville loped toward them, his tail wagging cautiously, nosing Otis up and down.

"I don't remember." Otis sat down on the floor and pulled off his borrowed running shoes.

Lissa's mom pulled a piece of paper off the fridge. "Look, here's a note. Only I can't read it in the dark. Otis, do you have a flash-light?"

Otis pulled one out of a drawer and to-gether they read the note, "Dear Otis and Lissa," it said. "I have gone to Windsor to-day to do some research before leaving for Collingwood tomorrow, but should be back in plenty of time for dinner. Dad."

Mom beamed the flashlight on her watch. "It's six-thirty. Why don't you leave a note for your dad and come to our house for dinner? He's probably been held up in traf-fic."

"Y-y-y-you don't think anything's hap-pened to him, do you?"

Mom flashed Lissa a look of warning. "Of course not. It's just the weather. The traf-fic lights are probably out and traffic's a mess. Come on. We'll light a fire in the fireplace and roast some wienies."

"I'll just feed Baskerville," said Otis, re-lief flooding his voice. Lissa squeezed her mom's hand.

Otis rattled off into the mud room and Baskerville followed him, his tail wagging in a slow and stately motion.

While her mom busied herself writing a

note for Otis's dad, Lissa sat at the stool in front of the iron stove and waited. She leaned back against the wall. Her whole body slumped as the events of the afternoon paraded through her mind. She shivered to think how close they'd come to disaster. Her hand fell off her lap as her chin fell sleepily toward her chest.

She jerked awake. Her hand was resting on a book that was stuffed under the cushion of the footstool. She stood and pulled it out from under her. It was a book called *Spirits of the Earth: A Guide to Native Symbols, Stories and Ceremonies*. She turned it over in her hand, remembering Otis telling her how his mom had had lots of different books in her library about what different tribes believed and how it was important to respect the beliefs of all.

Behind her she could hear Baskerville's dry dog food raining into his metal dish. Otis shut the door, and her mom finished writing the note. On impulse, Lissa stuffed the book under her sweater. She would read it later. Under the covers. After she'd gone to bed. Maybe it would help her understand a little more about some of the things Otis talked about.

The phone was ringing as they let themselves into Lissa's darkened house. Lissa's mom fumbled for the receiver and handed it to Otis with a big smile. "No worries, Otis. It's your dad."

"Dad?" Otis said in a small voice.

Lissa's mom smiled and flashed the light she'd brought along from Otis's so they could find their way into the house. "Come on, Lissa. Let's find some candles."

Lissa and her mom felt their way down the hall. Muggsy barked from far off in the house. He was probably hiding under Mom and Bill's bed, just like he had during the thunderstorm.

"Here, Muggsy," yelled Mom. He skittered into the kitchen, his nails clattering on the wooden floor, and washed Lissa with kisses while Mom rummaged around in the drawer. "Here we go," she said as she handed Lissa another flashlight. "You look in the fridge and find the hot dogs. I'll get a fire started."

Lissa crossed to the fridge and knelt down. "And Lissa," her mom said. "We're going to have a little talk about all this later."

Lissa gulped. Mom padded into the family room. Minutes later a crackling fire was burning brightly, sending out waves of warmth and cheer. Otis came into the kitchen.

"My dad's stuck in town," he said. "Some power lines are down and they've closed the highway. He says he'll be home as soon as he can, but he told me to thank you and your mom for bringing me here." Obviously Otis hadn't told his dad anything about the close call down at the lake.

With a sweep of yellow light, Bill's car pulled into the driveway.

Lissa's mom met him at the back door with the flashlight. Otis curled up in front of the fireplace with Muggsy nuzzling his palm, looking for a belly rub. Lissa used the chance to sneak away to her room. She put the spirits book under her pillow and went back downstairs.

"Hey, Lissa," said Bill when she came into the kitchen. "I hear you and Otis had quite an adventure today." His voice sounded serious.

"I told Bill we'd all have a long talk about it later," Mom said as she skewered the hot dogs onto straightened coat hangers. She wrapped the buns in some tin foil and carted it all into the family room.

After they'd eaten, Otis fell asleep on the floor, his head on a big pillow. The firelight flickered and danced, sending crazy shadows over his face. Even in his sleep he looked sad, like he was waiting for a bad dream. Although Lissa missed her dad, she was going to be seeing him soon. Suddenly it was good to know that he was still part of her life, even if she did live so far away. Every so often, her mom reached out and smoothed Lissa's hair. She couldn't imagine how sad it would be not to have her mom. And Monday she could sit with Julie at lunch. Just thinking about that made everything less lonely.

Mom and Bill sat on the couch, talking quietly, their voices soothing. Muggsy snored gently, every so often twitching and whining in his sleep. Lissa's eyelids grew heavy. Her mom reached over and touched Lissa's cheek. "It looks like Otis will be bunking here tonight. Why don't you go to bed, hon? If Mr. Striker doesn't get here in an hour or two, I'll pull out the hide-a-bed."

Lissa didn't need to be told twice. She kissed her mom goodnight. At the last second she even kissed Bill on the cheek. Bill was so surprised he jumped. "What's that for?" he asked.

Lissa shrugged. Bill wasn't her dad, but he was a good friend.

Mom smiled and squeezed Bill's hand. "We'll talk about all this tomorrow. Let's sleep on it. Unless there's something you want to tell me now?"

Lissa almost told her mom the whole story, but she was tired; Otis was safe and it looked like everything was going to be all right. "Nothing," she said.

Her mom opened her mouth as if to say something else, then decided against it.

"See you tomorrow, then."

"Come on Muggsy," Lissa said. Instantly, Muggsy was on his feet. Once in bed, Lissa pulled out the spirit book. The night seemed to have gotten even darker and fiercer. Without the heat of the fireplace, Lissa was cold. Muggsy tunneled his way under the covers and Lissa giggled when his wet nose brushed against her ankle. A pale white moon covered by tattered clouds shone weakly in the blowy night. The branches on the tree outside her window twisted and shook their bony claws at the sky. All at once Lissa wasn't tired anymore. She turned onto her side and stuffed her pillow against her cheek.

Lissa fished around for the flashlight she'd brought to bed with her, shone the light on the table of contents, and flipped to the chapter entitled, "Bird Signs and Omens." This wasn't a book about Ojibway traditions, Lissa saw. She wondered if Otis had noticed that. Still, she couldn't resist looking to see what the book would tell her about hawks. As she leafed through the pages, she saw the heading for the owl. Suddenly she remembered how an owl had swooped across her path the first night she went to Otis's house. Intrigued, Lissa began to read. "An owl is a bad sign and a bad power. It is a messenger of evil, sickness or a fatal accident." Like almost drowning? Lissa wondered. Underneath her covers, she shivered. Outside something tapped at her window and from the direction of her ankle, Muggsy whined nervously. Quickly she turned the page. What did the book say about hawks?

Lissa gasped. A hawk is considered a good bird and good power, but a very bad sign. It too warns of a dangerous or deadly accident.

Two birds, both warning of evil and danger. Suddenly, the wind died down.

And, in sudden quiet, Lissa's heard another noise, a noise like the flapping of wings. Startled she sat up in bed. On the swaying branch of the tree that reached across her window was framed the silhouette of a large bird. Its curved beak and glittering eyes were unforgettable.

It was Scarlett. Lissa was sure of it. Had the bird come to find Otis?

In the eerie stillness came the most spine-chilling sound Lissa had ever heard: the piercing scream of the hawk.

Chapter Ten

Lissa buried her head under the blanket. Under the covers, Muggsy woofed a low warning, and as quickly as it had appeared the hawk was gone. Lissa stared wide-eyed at the empty branch. Had she imagined it? The inky sky was empty but for slate-colored clouds and an orange moon surrounded by a faint silver glow. And hawks didn't fly at night, did they?

In her icy bedroom, Lissa's nose was as cold as Muggsy's. She thought longingly of the toasty warm fireplace and the comforting murmur of Mom's and Bill's voices. She had just decided to get up and tell them about what she'd seen, when she glanced at her bedside clock. Three thirty. How could that be? Hadn't she just come to bed?

She must have fallen asleep. One minute she'd been reading about the spirits of the earth, the next minute staring at a hawk on her tree branch. But Lissa knew she had gone to bed at ten thirty. She must have fallen asleep and dreamed the whole thing. The book she'd been reading was on the floor beside her bed. Lissa pressed the Indiglo button on her wristwatch: three thirty-three. She tried the switch on her bedside lamp. Had the power come back on? Nothing.

Lissa had never known the power to stay out for so long. She snuggled down under her covers and willed herself back to sleep. It felt good to be warm and comfortable while outside the wind blew and the night thickened and churned like the blackest lake water.

The next thing she knew, the clock said five thirty and a low humming noise told her the power was back on. The furnace rumbled away, filling the house with warmth, and Muggsy was at her window, whining in a low urgent voice.

Lissa jumped out of bed and crossed to the window. Dead tree branches were strewn across the lawn and the big old birch tree on the Maxwell's front lawn lay on its side, its roots writhing in the blowing wind like snakes in a pit. Across the street Lissa could make out Mr. Striker's car parked in the front driveway and a light on in the back kitchen. She breathed a sigh of relief. At least Otis's dad had made it home safely.

She pulled on her jeans, a heavy wool sweater and a pair of thick gym socks. Muggsy was waiting impatiently at her bedroom door. Mom and Bill were still fast asleep. Feeling a bit like she did on Christmas morning, Lissa tiptoed down the stairs. If she did nothing else today, Lissa was going to make sure Otis understood perfectly that he had to tell his father all about the hawk. It was more than the hawk, really. Otis needed to tell his father how he felt about missing his mom. And that was that.

Her mind made up, she opened the door of the family room. The fire had gone cold during the night, but Lissa could see where the couch had been pulled down and the cushions piled against the wall.

She peeked over the back of the couch and her breath caught in her throat. The bed was empty!

"Otis, stop kidding around," she said to the empty room. "I know you're here somewhere."

Nothing.

Maybe he was in the bathroom. Lissa hurried down the hall and knocked on the bathroom door. It swung open; the room was empty.

The kitchen! He was hungry and wanted some breakfast. He would be sitting at the kitchen table, wolfing down corn flakes. Lissa rounded the corner into the kitchen at a dead run, sliding on her stocking feet like she was stealing third base.

The kitchen was tidy. No empty cereal bowls cluttered the counter. No milk splashes on the floor. Just the refrigerator humming along. Muggsy scratched at the door to go out and Lissa let him into the back yard. She peered into the gloomy morning. It would be a couple more hours until the sun rose.

Then it hit her.

Mr. Striker had come home late last night, picked Otis up and taken him home.

The lights were on in the Striker's kitchen. Otis was probably spooning cereal down his throat right now.

That was it.

Why didn't she feel better?

Was it the fading memory of a strange bird sitting in her tree the night before?

Was it reading the animal spirit book and knowing that the owl and the hawk were both bad signs?

Or was it the nagging feeling that Otis hadn't really meant what he said when he promised not to run off by himself?

Muggsy appeared wet and doggy smelling at the back door. He nudged at the screen, wanting back in. Lissa stared at the Striker's big old house.

The decision made, she knelt and pulled on an old pair of rubber boots. She was going to go over to the Striker house and tell Otis how she felt. She drew on her rain parka and started across the street. Lights in houses along the way had started to come on, and Lissa knew Mom and Bill would be waking up soon. She broke into a jog.

Peering in through Otis's back porch window, she saw Baskerville snoozing in front of the cast iron stove. Under a pool of light from the chandelier, Mr. Striker sat reading a newspaper and sipping from a steaming cup. Otis was nowhere to be seen.

Lissa didn't like the way her stomach was lurching around inside her. She'd heard her grandmother talk about premonitions, about knowing something was going to happen *before* it actually does, but she'd never experienced the feeling herself. Until now. The little hairs on her arms were standing straight up like millions of antennae, just like in *The Secret in the Belfry* when the old lady felt a prickling on the back of her neck and then the box of poison was discovered under the eaves.

Mr. Striker looked up and saw her face in the window. For a minute he looked surprised; then he glanced over her shoulder as if he was expecting someone else.

That glance proved it.

Otis wasn't home either.

He was missing.

Chapter Eleven

"All right, Lissa, you better tell us everything you know."

Lissa's mom, Bill and Mr. Striker were standing in the hall of Lissa's house. Lissa was sitting on the bottom stair. Muggsy was leaning against her leg, offering moral support.

"Otis must be looking for the hawk."

"Explain, Lissa," said Mom, her face serious.

Lissa told them. Every detail. When she finished her eyes filled with tears.

"I'm sorry I didn't say something last night," she said.

Mr. Striker rubbed a hand across his face. "I should have suspected something like this might happen. He's been very secretive since his mother disappeared, always reading books from her library. Because of her Ojibway heritage, she was very interested in Aboriginal cultures and traditions and she told him a lot about different native beliefs and customs. But I never dreamed . . . " his voice trailed off.

"Do you have any idea where he might be, Lissa?" asked Bill. "I mean, where he might have gone to look for this hawk?"

"The only place I can think of is the marsh," she said. "Down at the lake, where the boathouse is."

"You mean where the hunters are?" Mr. Striker looked anxious.

"Yes," said Lissa. "That's where the hawk was when she disappeared."

"Show us," said Mom.

The lake was still shrouded in early morning fog and there was no sign of the sun. "I hope he's not wandering around down here," said Mr. Striker. "Even though hunting season won't start for a few weeks, there are always poachers out here. He could get shot by accident."

"Over there," said Lissa as they pulled into the parking lot. From the direction of the lake came the occasional sound of gunshots.

"Stay close to me, Lissa," said Mom as they made their way toward the dense growth that crowded the shoreline.

Their breath sent up puffs like smoke signals as they threaded their way down the path.

"I can't see two feet in front of me," said Bill.

"Careful," said Lissa. "There's a low hanging branch near the bridge . . . "

"Ouch!" said Bill rubbing his forehead. "Too late."

"Better let me go first. I remember the way from yesterday." Lissa stepped around Bill and into a giant puddle. The water was up to her knees.

By the time they reached the boathouse they were wet, muddy and very worried.

"Otis couldn't have come through this all by himself," said Lissa's mom. "He'd have gotten stuck."

"There it is!" said Lissa as the rickety wooden structure appeared through the trees.

"Do you see him?" yelled Mr. Striker as he strode through the tall grass and onto the dock.

"Otis!" he shouted into the wind. "Otis are you here?"

Silence. Her heart jumping, Lissa scanned the brackish water. Surely he wouldn't have fallen in again. She looked up and caught her mom doing the same thing. Their eyes met and Lissa could see fear in her mother's face.

This is all my fault, Lissa thought. I should have told the whole story last night. I never should have let Otis talk me into keeping his dumb old secret.

"He's not here," said Bill. He put his arm around Mr. Striker. "We better get home and call the police."

Lissa gulped. The police! The drive back to her house seemed to go on forever. No one spoke. Lissa stared out the window and tried to figure out where Otis would go. She went over all the things he had told her. None of it added up.

"Look!" said Bill. "There's a hawk trying to fly against the wind."

Lissa sat up and peered out the window.

It looked like the same bird that had been in her tree last night. What was it the book had said? *A good power, but a bad sign!*

Lissa suddenly knew that the bird had really appeared in her tree last night. She hadn't been imagining it. Nor had she been dreaming. The author of the book she had been reading had told of a time when a hawk had swooped down on his car as if trying to lift it in his talons. No one in the car had known the meaning of such behavior. Then the car had suddenly stopped. When the driver got out to check under the hood, the hawk had mysteriously reappeared and dropped a fish on the hood, causing the driver to jump back in surprise. At that moment the car's battery had exploded. The bird had saved his life. Maybe Otis was right. Maybe there were things in the world that couldn't be explained easily. Maybe the hawk really had been sent to look out for him.

Lissa watched the hawk wheeling and climbing in the sky until it flew away from the lake. It returned and climbed again.

The adults were captivated by the bird's strange behavior, but only Lissa suddenly realized what it meant.

"Follow the hawk, Mr. Striker," she said, pointing in the sky. "I think it's trying to tell us where Otis is."

"Don't be silly, hon," said Mom. "We need to get home and call the police."

"Every minute counts," Bill said.

"I know," said Lissa. "That's why we have to follow the hawk!" How could she make them understand?

"It's circling over our house," said Mr. Striker.

He was right. The bird was diving and climbing and diving again, as if it was pointing at something that was right under their noses.

Mr. Striker muttered, "It *is* over my house. Look!" He pointed to the sky where the bird had climbed again. "It's in the back, by the tree house."

Lissa and Mr. Striker spoke at the same time. "The tree house!"

The car sped through the streets. The darkness was fading to a thin, watery blue light. Another rainy day. Mr. Striker skidded into the driveway and was out of the car almost before it had come to a complete stop.

Overhead the hawk screamed and

careened in the wind currents. Lissa, Mom and Bill ran behind Mr. Striker across the deep wet grass, around the lilac hedge and behind the old rickety garden shed.

Lying beneath the tree house in the black walnut tree, face down and spread-eagled like a bat that had fallen from its perch, was Otis. His black cape billowed around him in the wind. The hawk perched on the broken branch that had held the old tree house. The wooden structure hung precariously half in and half out of the tree. With each gust of the wind, it shifted. A few boards were scattered around the ground.

"He's unconscious! He must have fallen out of the tree house when the branch broke! Help me move him before the whole tree house comes down on his head," yelled Mr. Striker.

Lissa's mom rushed forward. "Stabilize his neck," she said. Carefully Mom and Mr. Striker moved Otis to safety. "Bill, Lissa, go phone an ambulance," shouted Mom, her face pale as she reached for Otis's pulse.

Bill and Lissa ran for the house. With shaking fingers Lissa dialed 9-1-1, then handed the phone to Bill. He spoke to the operator in a calm, steady voice. Baskerville whined and pawed at the door.

"You better stay here, boy," Bill said. He and Lissa crossed the lawn together. As they got closer to where Otis was lying, Bill took her icy fingers in his. Lissa sobbed.

"It's all my fault."

"No, it's not, Lissa" Bill said. "You were just trying to be a friend to Otis. It looks like he needed a friend pretty bad."

Lissa rubbed the tears from her eyes, but more spilled over.

"I-I-I was going to tell him today that he had to talk to his d-d-dad."

Bill rubbed her shoulders. "He'll be all right. Don't blame yourself."

Easier said than done. Lissa stared at Otis's pale thin face. She wished she'd been a real friend instead of a pretend one.

The sound of a siren grew louder and a flashing red light on an ambulance appeared at the corner.

The attendants loaded Otis onto a stretcher and Mr. Striker climbed in behind. The doors closed and the ambulance pulled away.

"I'm just going to follow in the car," said

Lissa's mom. "I think Mr. Striker could use some company." She looked at Lissa's swollen eyes and red nose and said, "Don't worry, hon. He may have a broken arm and a slight concussion, but I think he's going to be fine."

In the black walnut tree, the hawk screamed and flapped her wings. Then she lifted off the branch and disappeared into the dawn sky.

"That's the strangest thing I ever saw," said Bill. "That bird led us right to him."

Mom nodded.

In her heart, Lissa said a silent thanks to Otis's guardian spirit.

Chapter Twelve

The small Windsor airport buzzed with people pulling suitcases, hugging friends goodbye and waiting at luggage carrousels.

Lissa jumped up and down as the plane taxied onto the runway.

"That's it. That's my plane."

"Have you got your boarding pass?" asked Mom. Lissa nodded and opened her backpack to show Mom the piece of paper safely stored right beside her wallet.

"Don't lose it!"

"I won't." Lissa craned her neck to see if the plane had stopped. People were coming down the portable steps and baggage handlers were unloading the luggage compartment.

"It won't be long now," said Bill.

The big day had finally arrived. Thanksgiving. Victoria! Danielle! Pumpkin carving! Dad! The list of fun and exciting things that she was going to do over the next week went on and on. Lissa skipped from foot to foot. It was better than Christmas morning, her birthday and Halloween all rolled into one!

The refueling truck had rolled out onto the runway. It wouldn't be long now.

Behind them, the door to the airport slid open and Mr. Striker, Otis and Julie came hurrying across the concourse.

"I was hoping you guys would make it in time!" said Lissa.

Mom and Bill smiled. Otis gestured with his cast. "It took longer for them to change it than we thought. Look, this one glows in the dark!"

Julie said, "He keeps dragging me into dark places so he can show it off!"

Lissa laughed.

"We brought you a going away present, Lissa," said Mr. Striker, handing Lissa a package.

"Open it," said Otis.

Lissa ripped off the wrapping paper, revealing a small blue box. Inside was a beautiful silver charm shaped like a hawk in full flight.

"We thought you could wear it on your chain — right next to your medallion that says 'best,'" said Julie. "So you don't forget us when you're away."

"Thanks, you guys," said Lissa. "It's beautiful." She slipped it on the chain and fastened it around her neck.

"Now you have a guardian spirit too," said Otis.

Lissa gave him a hug. He blushed. Julie punched him playfully in his good arm.

"Otis is going to teach me some of his magic tricks while you're gone," said Julie. "Then when you come back I can help put on magic shows for birthday parties too."

Lissa smiled. It was so exciting. After Otis had been released from the hospital the day after he'd fallen out of the tree house, he had begun teaching Lissa and Julie his magic tricks. Word had gotten around and they'd been asked to perform at Julie's little brother's birthday. They'd been such a hit that they had three more parties booked already.

"My dad's going to teach me some more tricks while you're away," said Otis. "He used to put on magic shows when he was in college."

"Like father, like son." Mr. Striker laughed.

Otis leaned against his dad, and Mr. Striker hugged him. "Otis is going to keep me company on that research trip I had to postpone."

"Yeah, we're going spelunking!"

Lissa shivered. Otis and his dad had changed in some ways. But some things stayed the same. They were always going to be weird. But then, Lissa had decided that weird was very definitely absolutely interesting.

"And then we're going to go and visit Otis's grandfather on Manitoulin Island. I think it's about time he understood more about his Ojibway heritage. Right, Otis?"

Otis nodded.

"Time to go, Liss," said Bill.

"Have a great trip, hon," said Mom. "Don't forget to give Danielle my love."

Everyone gave her a hug — even Otis.

"Thank you for everything you've done, Lissa," Mr. Striker said. He smiled at Otis. "We owe you a lot."

As she climbed onto the plane, Lissa had a startling thought.

Even though it was good to be going on a visit, she was looking forward to coming home — home to Mom and Bill and Muggsy and Otis and Julie.

Home to Harmony Beach.

Nancy Belgue went to six different schools before beginning the eighth grade. Her mother's favorite line when Nancy was growing up was "adversity builds character," usually delivered along with the news of another move. When Nancy's younger son had to start grade six in a new town, she remembered how hard it was to be the new kid, and *The Scream of the Hawk* was begun. The plot thickened when she realized that she lives in one of the prime paths taken by migrating hawks. *The Scream of the Hawk* is her first novel.